MARKUS AND THE GIRLS

MARKUS + THE GIRLS

Klaus Hagerup

TRANSLATED BY Tara Chace

Front Street
Honesdale, Pennsylvania

Originally published in Norway in 1997 by H. Aschehoug & Co.
under the title *Markus og jentene*
Copyright © 1997, 2003 by H. Aschehoug & Co. (W. Nygaard), Oslo
English translation copyright © 2009 by Tara Chace
All rights reserved
Printed in China
Designed by Helen Robinson
First U.S. edition, 2009

This translation has been published with the financial support of NORLA.

LIBRARY OF CONGRESS CATALOGING-IN-PUBLICATION DATA
Hagerup, Klaus.
[Markus og jentene. English]
Markus and the girls / Klaus Hagerup ;
translated by Tara Chace. — 1st U.S. ed.
p. cm.
Summary: Only two months into his first year of junior high school,
Markus has already fallen in love with all of the girls in his class.
ISBN-13: 978-1-59078-520-1 (hardcover : alk. paper)
[1. Love—Fiction. 2. Junior high schools—Fiction.
3. Schools—Fiction. 4. Norway—Fiction. 5. Humorous stories.]
I. Chace, Tara. II. Title.
PZ7.H12425Me 2009
[Fic]—dc22
2007048850

FRONT STREET
An Imprint of Boyds Mills Press, Inc.
815 Church Street
Honesdale, Pennsylvania 18431

MARKUS AND THE GIRLS

CHAPTER 1

"What, again?" Sigmund exclaimed, concerned. "It just isn't normal, Wormster."

"I can't help it, Sigmund. It just sort of keeps happening."

"Nothing just happens. You have free will, don't you?"

"I don't think so."

"Of course you do. Otherwise you'd just be wandering around."

"Isn't that what I'm doing?"

"There must be something wrong with your pituitary gland."

"Yeah," Markus said and sighed. "That's what I figure."

"First it was Ellen Christine, then it was Beate, then it was Karianne, then it was Mona, then it was Hanne, then it was Hilde, then it was Turid, then it was Ellen, then it was Lise, then it was Anne Berit. …"

"No, then it was Heidi."

"No. Heidi was *after* Anne Berit."

"She was?"

"Yes, she was." Sigmund said, and looked at him sternly. "Then it was Trude, then it was Elisabeth, then it was Therese. I mean, that's like pretty much every girl in our class. So who is it now?"

"Now it's Ellen Christine."

"Ellen Christine? What, again?"

"Yeah," Markus said quietly. "She has such pretty ears. I didn't notice them the first time."

Markus Simonsen was in love. For the fifteenth time since starting junior high. And that was two months ago.

"Do you think I'm a nymphomaniac, Sigmund?"

Sigmund nodded somberly. "I'm afraid you might be."

"But I'm only thirteen," Markus whispered hoarsely. "What am I going to do if it stays like this?"

"Castration is an option, of course," Sigmund said slowly.

"Sigmund!"

"It's a simple surgical procedure. We got our cat castrated last week. It made him completely calm, and he stopped spraying."

"I don't spray!"

"No, not yet, but just wait."

"How do you know that?"

"I know what I know," Sigmund said, blushing.

"I don't want to be castrated!"

"Relax. I was only kidding."

"That's not something to kid around about. That's terrible!"

Markus looked up at Sigmund in desperation. They were walking side by side on the little gravel path home from school. Sigmund was tall, dark-haired, and elegant, and Markus was short, blond, and inelegant. It was really windy, one of those fall storms that always made Markus feel like any minute he would be able to fly.

"So, help me, Sigmund. Tell me what I should ... Oh no, here she comes!" He tried to hide behind Sigmund's back.

"Who?"

"Ellen Christine!"

She was running down the path with Mona. They were wearing

short leather jackets, tight pants, and suede shoes. Ellen Christine's hair was fluttering in the wind so that Markus and Sigmund could see her ears. They were small, and they stuck out a little bit. And they were quite red because it was so windy and cold out.

"Hey, Ellen Christine!" Sigmund yelled.

"Hey!"

Markus pulled his jacket up over his head and buttoned it shut. The girls stopped and waved at them.

"Hi, Sigmund!" Mona called. "Isn't it awesome that it's Friday?"

"Yeah," Sigmund yelled. "And you really can't complain about the weather, can you?"

"We sure can't," Ellen Christine yelled. "We're going to a handball game! What happened to Markus's head?"

"His ears got cold," Sigmund yelled.

The girls waved and ran off down the path. Markus kept standing there with his head in his jacket.

"You can come out now, Wormster. They're gone."

A pale face slowly emerged from the down jacket. "Oh my God, Sigmund! Did you see those ears?"

"What's so special about them?"

"Couldn't you see that they're different?" Markus whispered, excited.

"All ears are different," Sigmund said condescendingly. "Unless they're cloned."

"Didn't you see how they look like ... mussels?"

"Mussels?"

"Yes, like mussels with pearls."

"Pearls?"

"Yeah, her earrings are exactly like those freshwater pearls that grow in mussels."

"There's no way you could've seen her earrings all the way from here."

"No, but I noticed them in last period at school. I was looking at them the whole time. While we were writing our essays."

"How were you able to write, then?"

"She inspired me. I wrote about a young man who was diving for pearls in the Maldives. He met a mermaid underwater with pearl mussels for ears."

"Mermaids don't have mussels for ears," Sigmund said.

Markus looked at him in surprise. "Um, hello? Mermaids don't even exist in the first place."

"You never know," Sigmund said curtly.

"Well, then you can't know if they have mussels for ears either."

"You can pretty much figure they don't," Sigmund said a little snootily.

"But they have fish tails, right?"

"That's the theory, yes."

"I don't give a damn about theory," Markus said grumpily.

"I know. That's why you're so bad at math."

"I am not. I got a B+ on the last test."

"And I got an A+," Sigmund said, sounding smug.

Markus wondered for a second whether he ought to keep going with this conversation, but he knew that no matter how long they keep going, Sigmund wouldn't give in until he'd had the last word. Besides, Markus's head was still filled with thoughts of Ellen Christine's amazing ears, so he let it go. "Anyway, it's the best essay I've ever written in my whole life!"

Sigmund smiled—the smile he always wore when he felt like he'd won a debate. Markus acted like he didn't notice. "The young man and the mermaid get together down there at the bottom of the ocean. They get married and have children."

"How many?"

"A school," Markus said.

"A school?"

"Yeah, I mean she's half fish, right? So they have a school of children."

"No one has a school of children, Markus. It's totally unrealistic."

"It's just a *little* school," Markus mumbled, thinking that actually a lot of things about the scenario were unrealistic. It was unrealistic that the boy would survive down there at the bottom of the ocean, it was unrealistic that they had a wedding down there, and it was unrealistic that anyone could have children with a mermaid at all. Because if the mermaid were half fish, Markus couldn't understand how it would be possible for them to have children. Actually, the idea that they would have a school of children, if they could even reproduce in the first place, might be the most realistic part of the whole thing.

"A school is a school," Sigmund said.

"It doesn't matter anyway," Markus said in exasperation. "What matters is that I wrote it out of love."

"For the mermaid?"

"No! For Ellen Christine. I love her, Sigmund. What am I going to do?"

"Tell her that you love her, I suppose."

"Are you crazy?"

"Show her your essay, then."

"Huh?"

"Tell her that she inspired you to write it."

"She'll just laugh at me."

"Not if the essay is good. And the school of children isn't too big," he added thoughtfully.

"I wouldn't dare. You have to help me, Sigmund!"

Sigmund frowned. He knew that made him look even wiser than he was. "OK, Wormster," he said slowly. "*I'll* do it."

"Do what?"

"I'll show her the essay and tell her I wrote it. If she laughs at me, I'm strong enough to take it. If she doesn't …"

"If she doesn't …?"

"Then I'll tell her that you wrote it and then you …"

Markus looked at him expectantly. "And then I what?"

"Then you have yourself a pearl," Sigmund said.

It was Monday. The bell had rung after last period. Sigmund had caught Ellen Christine and said that he'd written an essay he really wanted her to hear. Now she was sitting on a trash can in the school-yard, and with her eyes wide and her mouth hanging open, she was staring at Sigmund, who was standing in front of her and reading.

Markus was standing a few yards away, pretending he was looking for something in his backpack, but he heard every word, even though that wasn't necessary. He knew the whole thing by heart. If he hadn't been so nervous, he would have been impressed, because Sigmund read it extremely well, almost like an actor. Which wasn't surprising, because Sigmund didn't want to be an astrophysicist anymore when he grew up. He wanted to be an actor and had performed for Markus the Buckride scene—the dramatic tale of the reindeer hunt—from the beginning of *Peer Gynt*. That had been no joke. He'd read the scene with such fierce fervor, and when he bellowed that he was about to plunge the knife into the reindeer's throat, he was staring at Markus with a look that almost made him believe Sigmund was going to plunge the butter knife into his throat. His reading now was just as convincing. Low and intense, his eyes focused intently on Ellen Christine's. Markus was totally sure he saw two tears run down her cheeks. He was only barely able to stop himself from crying, because this was one of the most beautiful stories he'd ever heard in his life:

"The young man let his fingers glide cautiously over the lovely mermaid's right ear. 'Did you know,' he said softly, 'that it was your ears I fell for?' They were all alone. All of their little children were off exploring a coral reef. They were delightful children and always playing practical jokes. They looked like their mother and had their father's adventurous spirit. She smiled at him but didn't say anything.

'Have I told you that they look like mussels?' he whispered.

She nodded. Her long, wet hair swaying around her like jellyfish tentacles, except jellyfish have stingers. The mermaid didn't. She was perfect, an ocean princess, and she was his.

'I have a present for you,' he said softly.

'Oh, Sigurd!'

He took two milky white pearls out of the pocket in his swim trunks.

The beautiful mermaid squealed with delight and clapped her hands in the slow, smooth motions that he would never get tired of watching.

'Pearls for me?'

'Yes,' he whispered. 'Pearls for you, my own beloved little mussel.'

He attached them carefully to her ears and held her hand.

'Where are we going?' she asked quietly.

'Far away and farther than far,' he answered calmly. 'Out to the horizon. Where the ocean melts into the sunrise.'

She looked into his eyes and laughed happily."

Sigmund rubbed his eyes with a quick, slightly awkward motion that Markus couldn't even tell was awkward. It was coldly calculating. Sigmund flashed Ellen Christine a sly, shy smile.

"Well," he said cheerfully, "that was the essay. What did you think?"

"It was … totally … amazing," Ellen Christine whispered.

"It was written for you," Sigmund said quietly.

"Huh?"

"It's a tribute to your ears."

Markus felt himself grow burning hot. Wasn't Sigmund going a little too far now?

"My ears?"

"Yes, you have the most beautiful ears in the world."

"I do?" Ellen Christine's voice was so quiet that Markus almost couldn't hear what she was saying.

"Yes, Ellen Christine. They look like mussels."

Sigmund was still smiling. Ellen Christine sat still for a second. Then she leaned forward, kissed Sigmund quickly on the cheek, hopped down from the trash can, and ran across the schoolyard over to Mona, who was standing near the bike rack.

"Whoa," Markus said.

Sigmund turned around. He had two red blotches on his cheeks and his eyes were sort of distant.

"I think she liked it," he said slowly.

"Yes, I noticed that, too. Why—"

"I think I did the text justice."

"Well, yeah, but—"

"Not sentimental, but not dry either. Did you notice how intense I was?"

"Well, yeah, Sigmund. But you should—"

"And at the same time I was totally relaxed. That's the trick, Markus. The audience has to get wrapped up in what's going on, not the actors. I used the same technique as Leonardo DiCaprio."

"Well, yeah, I get that, but why didn't you say I wrote it?"

Sigmund looked at him in astonishment. "Are you crazy? That would ruin everything."

"Well, but …"

"If there's one thing I've learned as an actor," Sigmund said, staring dreamily out into space, "it's never reveal your secrets to the audience."

"But, um, that was the whole point."

"What was?"

"If she liked it, you were going to tell her that I was the one who wrote it."

"I was?"

"Yes!"

Sigmund was starting to look normal again. "I'll do it tomorrow, Wormster. Let me bask in the pleasure of my success for a few more hours."

"Well, all right," Markus mumbled. "But tomorrow you'd better tell her."

Sigmund nodded.

"For sure?"

Sigmund nodded again. "Far away and farther than far," he said calmly. "Out to the horizon. Where the ocean melts into the sunrise."

CHAPTER 2 "Dad, have you ever been in love?"

Markus and Mons were each leaning against a tree, stretching. They'd started going for jogs together in the woods just behind their house. Markus didn't actually like jogging, but he did it every Monday now to make his dad happy. He knew that it made Mons feel like he wasn't just Markus's father but also his friend, and he knew that his dad had a secret dream that Markus would become such a good runner that he would become an Olympic champion. Mons had dreamed of doing that himself once, but the best he'd done was fifth place in the 60-meter sprint in a regional competition. Now he was standing by the tree, sweating and breathing hard and happily.

"In love? You bet I have, sure," he said with a manly laugh. "I was so in love that I almost lost my mind, and you should be glad I was. Otherwise you wouldn't be here." He winked at Markus. A friendly wink. It was obvious that he had liked the question. A jog with his best friend. A sweaty forehead. Pine needles in his hair. Dirty jogging shoes. The woods and guy talk. Yes, siree.

"I didn't mean Mom," Markus said. "I meant before."

"Before Mom?" Mons wiped his forehead. "No … oh yeah, as a matter of fact when I was in high school there was a girl who … But nothing ever came of that. She was together with Guttorm."

Guttorm was Mons's best friend when he was a little. Guttorm was a bit of a ladies' man. Just like Sigmund, Markus thought, feeling a little pang in his side. He'd had a stitch in his side when they were jogging and it was probably back now even though he was standing still. You just never know with a stitch.

"Just one?"

Mons wiped his forehead again. There sure was a lot of sweat there. "Yup, that's it," he said cheerfully. "To be honest, I wasn't exactly a Casanova. Why are you asking about this?"

"No reason."

"Markus?"

"Yeah, Dad?"

"Are you in love?"

Markus went back to stretching with all his might. His thighs burned. "No," he mumbled, "of course not."

"Have you ever been in love, then?"

One lie is all right, but two is starting to become a habit, Markus thought.

"I may have," he said as generally as he could.

"It's nothing to be embarrassed about. It's totally natural."

"Yeah," Markus mumbled, "that's what I figure."

"Was she pretty?"

Markus nodded and thought that he should never have brought it up. Mons might possibly be the world's most curious dad, and he surely wouldn't give up until he found out the age, hair color, eye color, height, and weight of the girl.

"What was her name?"

"Oh, I don't remember," Markus said.

"You don't remember?" Mons said, astonished.

Markus shook his head. What was he supposed to say? That her name was Ellen Christine, Beate, Karianne, Mona, Hilde, Hanne, Turid, Ellen, Lise, Anne Berit, Heidi, Trude, Elisabeth, Therese, and now it was Ellen Christine again? Dad would think he was sick, and he was, too. Sick with love. Crazed! Insatiable! Desperate! Ravenous! Frisky Markus! Little Markus the Rabbit. That was him! He'd wondered if he had inherited this disease from his father, but Mons had been in love only one time before Mom, and it was with Guttorm's girlfriend. And he certainly hadn't gotten it from Mom. She'd been warm, secure, and calm. No, neither Mom nor Dad had suffered from this terrible, unfortunate love disease. Just *him*.

"What about after?" It was the last possible straw, but Markus was clinging to it.

"After what?"

"After Mom. Have you been in love with anyone since Mom?"

Mons pulled a pine needle out of his hair and picked his teeth with it. "No, of course I haven't," he said, looking off into the trees. "Of course I haven't been in love with anyone since Mom."

They kept stretching. Neither of them said anything. Markus thought how some days fall felt more like fall than other days. He glanced over at Mons, who was stretching with one foot braced against the tree trunk. A little bit of white skin bulged out between the top and the pants of his red tracksuit. He's put on weight, Markus thought. He was thinner when Mom was alive.

Mons brought his leg down from the tree and turned toward Markus. He'd been far away. Now he was back again. "Do you know why I fell in love with your mother?" he asked cheerfully.

"No."

"Because of her index finger."

Markus held his breath, waiting.

"Do you remember how her right index finger was missing a joint?"

Markus nodded.

"She got it pinched in a door when she was little."

"I remember that," Markus said, realizing he had goose bumps.

"She told me that when she applied for a job with us. 'I can't bend it,' she said, 'but I'm a pretty good typist anyway.' And then she gave me the finger."

"What?"

Mons laughed. "I didn't mean it like that. She held her finger out to me and let me feel it, too, and that's when I knew."

"What did you know, Dad?" Markus asked, rejoicing on the inside.

"I knew that she was going to be your mother."

He reached his arm out toward Markus and pulled a few pine needles out of his hair.

"I'll race you!" Markus yelled. "Last one to the rock is a rotten egg, Dad! On your mark, get set, go!" He started running and heard Dad's voice behind him.

"OK, come on! I'm going to beat you this time, Vebjørn Rodal."

And some days fall feels less like fall than others, Markus thought.

Markus was so nervous he tripped. Sigmund was going to tell Ellen Christine who wrote the essay today. Sigmund figured that once she knew who the mermaid was, she would also figure out who the young man was. If Sigmund was right, it would melt Ellen Christine's heart and her beautiful ears would be Markus's. Maybe forever. But he was starting to have doubts. He felt like he had to go to the bathroom, the way he often did when he was nervous. Maybe she didn't like the essay anymore and had started thinking about other things besides the mermaid's beautiful ears. The tail, for example. It might not be so nice to be compared to a creature that's half fish. And what about the school of children? Obviously Sigmund was right. No one had a school of children, and if someone did, surely it wouldn't be that much fun, especially not for the mother. Maybe she thought the whole thing was just some sort of subtle teasing. And what would he do if she actually did fall in love with him? Hold her hand? Kiss her? Go swimming? And what would he talk to her about? He wasn't exactly a world champion when it came to talking to girls he was in love with. Usually he couldn't manage to say anything, and if he did manage, his voice was so strange and weak. It didn't remind him of Leonardo DiCaprio's voice. It was more like Donald Duck's voice. And *that* voice didn't usually make much of an impression on the girls.

He glanced up at Sigmund. "Today's the day, man," he said and noticed that he was starting to get the Donald Duck voice already.

Sigmund looked over toward the school. His eyes had that faraway look. "Did you know," he said softly, "that it was your ears I fell for?"

"Huh?"

Sigmund looked at him thoughtfully. "You're right, Wormster. She's got pretty nice ears."

When they got to school, Ellen Christine wasn't there. Mona said that she had a fever and had to stay home for three days at least. The first thing Markus felt was relief, but that didn't last long. Why did she get sick right now? Was the essay so good that it fired up her whole body, chaining her to her bed in a fever of passion? It would certainly be a bit of a downer then when she found out that it was written by a perky little guy with a Donald Duck voice. He felt the pressure in his stomach and rushed downstairs to the bathroom. He was in there for a while. When he came back up again, Sigmund was still standing there talking to Mona.

"Sure," he said. "I will."

"You will what?" Markus asked.

"Give her a copy of the essay," Sigmund said. "I'm going to stop by her place with it this afternoon."

"Oh," Markus said indifferently. "So did Ellen Christine like it?"

Mona smiled at him. Come to think of it, she had very pretty teeth.

"She thinks it's the most amazing thing she's heard in her whole life. She asked if Sigmund would come and read it to her again."

"I'd be delighted to," Sigmund said in a Leonardo DiCaprio voice.

"Aren't you afraid you'll catch whatever she has?" Markus asked, his voice a little hoarse.

"Sure," Sigmund said calmly, "but that's a chance I'll have to take."

"It's super nice of you, Sigmund," Mona said, and smiled again.

Markus noticed that one of her front teeth was slightly crooked. "Tell her I said hi and get well soon," he said.

Mona looked at him and asked, "Do you have a cold or something, Wormster?"

"Heh, heh," Markus croaked, wondering if he should give up talking for good.

Then, luckily, the bell rang for their first class.

"Hi."

Sigmund was standing outside the front door, smiling a strange, slightly foolish smile.

"Did you go?"

"Yeah."

"How did it go?"

"Good."

Mons peeked out at them from the living room. "Hi, Sigmund, is that you?"

"It is indeed, Mr. Simonsen," Sigmund said politely. "I'm me and you're you. That's how we're able to tell people apart from each other."

Mons mumbled something or other and disappeared into the living room again.

"What did she say?" Markus asked.

"She said thanks."

"When?"

"When I gave her the essay."

"You mean when you told her I was the one who wrote it."

Sigmund looked down at the doormat. "Well …," he said.

"Well?"

"Well, it turns out that …" Sigmund said, scratching his cheek. He seemed almost shy.

"Just say it," Markus said. "She doesn't love me."

"Noooo …," Sigmund said slowly. Now he was smiling that foolish smile again. "Actually, she loves … me."

Markus felt his knees beginning to quiver. "You!"

"Yes, Markus. I'm sorry." He didn't exactly look like he was sorry.

"How can she love you?"

"I think," Sigmund said thoughtfully, "that it has something to do with my personality."

"But what about the essay?"

"I think that also contributed to triggering her feelings," Sigmund said cheerfully. "Thanks."

"Thanks for what?"

"For bringing us together."

"I brought you together?!" Markus yelled. "I was the one who … You said that she would fall in love with me when you told her that I was the one who wrote it."

"Well, it turns out," Sigmund repeated, "that I never exactly told her you were the one who wrote it."

"Huh?"

"I was afraid it would break her heart."

"What are you talking about?"

"Well, she was already in love with me, wasn't she? If I told her it was your essay, she would have felt bad because she couldn't reciprocate your love."

Markus just looked at him.

"She's very sensitive, Markus. She would've been crushed between the guilt of not being able to return your affections for her and her love for me, and I know you wouldn't want to subject her to that. You of all people. And then there's one other thing. ..."

Markus didn't say anything. He knew what Sigmund was going to say before the words even came out.

"I love her, too, and it's your fault," Sigmund added, almost reproachfully.

"My fault?!"

"Yes," said Sigmund. "You were the one who pointed out her ears to me."

He put his hand on Markus's shoulder. It weighed a couple of tons. "Thank you so much, Markus."

There were thousands of things Markus wanted to say. He was standing face-to-face with the most devious guy he'd ever met. A despicable traitor he had trusted and confided in. A jerk who would sell out even his best friend. Mostly he wanted to start crying, but his eyes were dry; his chest, filled with granite; his thoughts, a black hole.

"Thanks a lot, you bastard," he said and shut the door so he didn't have to look at the face of his disloyal former friend anymore.

CHAPTER 3

Markus woke up with the feeling that something was wrong. At first he couldn't remember what it was, but then it sank in him like a stone. It was Sigmund! Sigmund the shifty! Sigmund the sneaky! Sigmund the scrounger! He'd lost his best friend. His childhood was over. From now on, life would be just one long, terrible fight about women. Where friendship didn't matter. Where no trick was too dirty. Where anything went. Where the law of the jungle prevailed. A lone wolf, that's what he was. He closed his eyes. He wanted to sleep. For a hundred years. He tried to think about nothing, but couldn't do it. It was as if Sigmund's foolish smile had forced its way into his brain and the slavering, gaping mouth was sucking out all his thoughts.

They'd been friends for ten years. And they'd been ten good years. They'd played together when they were little, and when Sigmund wanted to be an astrophysicist, he'd taught Markus lots of interesting stuff about the solar system. They'd formed secret clubs, and when Markus got teased for being such a fraidycat, Sigmund had defended him. In word and deed. "Word and deed." A typical Sigmund expression. Markus would never have come up with a thought like that on his own. Their friendship had been so strong that Sigmund had almost become a part of him. Even now after the betrayal, he thought Sigmund's thoughts. "In word and deed." But now it was over.

Now he was alone, and Sigmund was probably off somewhere, sucking the heck out of Ellen Christine's ears. Ellen Christine and those ridiculous ears of hers. Mussels? Oh no. Cauliflower was more like it! Snail shells! Chanterelle mushrooms! Good-bye love. For some strange reason he felt a little pang of guilt. This was the first time since he woke up that he'd thought about Ellen Christine. It was kind of like she'd gotten lost. His thoughts about her had been drowned out by his thoughts about Sigmund. Even though Ellen Christine was the one he was in love with.

"I mean, it's not like I love Sigmund," he whispered.

"What did you say?"

Mons had come in to wake him up.

"I mean, it's not like I love Sigmund," Markus said out loud.

"Well, *that* would certainly make things a little more complex," Mons said, setting a glass of milk on his nightstand. "Why do you say that?"

"I was just talking to myself," Markus mumbled, taking the glass of milk.

Mons stood there for a second, watching him in concern. It looked as if he were searching for something to say, but the only thing he came up with was "The milk is cold."

But by then Markus had already turned around so he was facing the wall.

"Yes, well, anyway now, it's morning," his dad said quietly and slipped out of the room.

The day turned into exactly the nightmare Markus had known it would. Even though he left his house ten minutes later than usual, Sigmund was waiting for him down by the intersection as if it were a completely normal day. He was even smiling.

"Hi, Wormster," he said. "How's it going?"

Markus didn't respond. He gazed randomly up at a tree by the intersection, stumbled on a rock, fell over, put his hands out to stop the fall, got back up onto his feet again, and limped along as quickly as he could with a sprained ankle. It really hurt, but he didn't say anything.

"Did you hurt yourself?" Sigmund had come up next to him and held out his hand to help. Markus wondered for a second if he ought to spit on it, but he didn't. That would mean showing his feelings, and Markus had decided never to show Sigmund a single one of his feelings again. Feelings were for humans, and Sigmund was not even human. He was air; no, he wasn't even that. He was a glob of flesh walking around polluting the air Markus was breathing.

"Does it hurt?"

Markus bit his lip. If he bit hard enough, maybe that would hurt so much he would forget about the pain from his ankle. It didn't work. Now both his ankle and his lip hurt. What he really wanted to do was run, away from this flesh glob's fake sympathy, but that wasn't possible. His ankle was definitely swelling now, and if he kept walking on it, it was sure to get even worse. It might need to be amputated. It didn't matter anyway. They could amputate his whole body if they wanted.

"Your lip is bleeding!"

Markus stared down at the path, but Sigmund's worried face was stuck, like a bit of dust, in the corner of his eye. He wished he had blinders on, like a horse. Then he wouldn't have to see anything he didn't want to see.

"Markus, you could at least say something!"

He stopped and turned toward the glob of flesh.

They looked each other in the eye for a second. Markus was filled with a woozy nausea. It was as if he were standing on the top of a cliff and looking down at a river way down below him. He had an intense, aching need to let himself fall over forward, down into the river. He only just barely kept himself from grabbing onto Sigmund to steady himself, but he stayed on his feet and his voice sounded dry and strange when he said, "Who are you?"

"Huh?" Sigmund gave him a confused look. Then he smiled. "You mean philosophically?" he asked.

Sometimes the most intelligent people are the dumbest ones, Markus thought. Sigmund was good at math and analyzing things and debating, but he didn't understand anything.

"In that case," Sigmund continued, "I'd have to say that I ..."

"You don't have to say anything," Markus said, staring down the road again. "I don't know you."

In the distance he saw Ellen Christine. She was standing on the sidewalk, looking over at them. No, not at them. At Sigmund. Cauliflower Ears and Glob of Flesh—the world's stupidest couple. He should write an essay about them, and in the essay they'd both end up at the dump. Now she was waving. Out of the corner of his eye he saw that Sigmund's face was red as he ran past Markus and over to Ellen Christine. He looked almost embarrassed, but Markus knew that he wasn't. He was just in love. But it didn't matter anymore what he was. Embarrassed or in love. Dumb or smart. Grumpy or happy. There were millions of people in the world that Markus didn't know. One more or one less wasn't going to matter. He started walking down the road again. His ankle didn't hurt anymore now, just his head. Ellen Christine took Sigmund's hand. It wouldn't be long before they started kissing each other and worse. Maybe she'd get pregnant, too. That would make a great headline in *Se og Hør*, Norway's premier celebrity news and gossip magazine: "Underage Girl Knocked Up by Same-Age Hooligan." Guess who wouldn't be sticking up for his former friend then?

"'Unfortunately that guy has always been a creep,'" Markus Simonsen said in an exclusive interview with *Se og Hør*. "'He should've been castrated a long time ago. He's technically a nymphomaniac.'"

Markus made a *tsk-tsk-tsk* sound through his clenched teeth as he watched Sigmund and Ellen Christine disappear into the front door of the school and out of his life.

Markus and Sigmund sat in the back two seats over by the windows. They'd sat there ever since elementary school. It was like those were their own private seats, and no one had protested when Sigmund asked if they could hold on to them in junior high. They didn't cause trouble and didn't talk much during class, but they'd taught themselves Morse code. Markus sent secret signals to Sigmund by poking him in the back with his pencil, and Sigmund responded by tapping Markus's foot, which was always stretched out under Sigmund's desk. Now and then they passed each other notes. They'd developed elegant techniques to keep other people from finding out. That's how they made the time pass, even in classes with Mr. Hansen, who was so boring that half the students were usually snoring when they were supposed to be saying grace before a snack or singing "O thee who feeds the little bird. Bless our food. O God."

Today Markus sat with his legs tucked underneath his own chair and just watched while Sigmund tried to reach them with his foot. When he almost made it, Markus pulled his legs back even further. Sigmund bent forward while holding onto his desk and stretched his legs as far back as he could. Markus moved his chair back, and Sigmund stretched even further. Ellen and Turid, who sat next to them, had noticed what was going on. They were watching Sigmund while trying not to giggle without making any noise. Their English teacher, Mr. Waage, had also noticed that something strange was going on back in the corner. He turned around at the blackboard, where he'd been writing out vocabulary words, and peered with interest at the boy whose posture was starting to look more and more like a ski jumper in midflight. The rest of the class had gotten very quiet. The only person who didn't notice that something was wrong was Sigmund, because he was totally preoccupied with finding the feet behind him so he could send his message to Markus in Morse code.

Mr. Waage cleared his throat. "Hello, back there!" he said.

Right then, Markus raised his right foot under his desk and kicked Sigmund in the calf as hard as he could.

"Ouch!" Sigmund squeaked and pulled his leg back, tipping over his chair and falling onto the floor. His chin cracked against the edge of the desk, and his teeth almost severed the tip of his tongue.

"What the …!" he yelled.

"What did you say?" Mr. Waage's voice sounded quite severe.

"Nudding. I juss bid my dongue," Sigmund mumbled.

Ellen and Turid were laughing out loud. Sigmund had turned red all the way down his neck. Markus glanced over at Ellen Christine. She looked like she was on the verge of laughing herself. Typical girl, he thought. First they hold your hand and then they laugh at you behind your back. And to think he'd been in love with her. Phew! Good luck in hell, Sigmund!

"Perhaps this kind of situation could be avoided if you try and sit in the chair normally," Mr. Waage said.

Sigmund nodded. Markus pretended he didn't see the sad puppy-dog eyes Sigmund was sending his way.

"Nineteen, nineteen, nineteen and a half," whispered Reidar as if scoring a ski jump.

Someone laughed.

"No," Markus said loudly. "Nine, nine, nine and a half. He fell."

Even Mr. Waage laughed. "Funny, Markus," he said in English, trying to get the students back on topic. "Don't you think Markus is a funny guy, Sigmund?"

"Yes, he is very funny," Sigmund answered in English. He wasn't laughing.

"OK, people," Mr. Waage said. "Can anyone give me some synonyms for the word 'funny'?"

And while the classroom buzzed with voices calling out "amusing," "hilarious," "humorous," "comical," "entertaining," and a number of other more-or-less-correct English words for "funny," Sigmund wrote a few words on a slip of paper. He dropped it on the floor and kicked it back toward Markus, who picked it up.

"Teacher, I found a piece of paper on the floor," Markus said.

"Oh, did you now?" Mr. Waage said in Norwegian, intrigued. "This certainly seems to be an interesting class period." Then he said the same thing again in English, because he hadn't forgotten for a second that he was here to teach these young rascals English. "Give it to me, Markus."

Markus got up and walked up to the chalkboard. Sigmund had slumped down in his desk with his head in his hands. "Vær så god, lærer," Markus said in Norwegian, handing him the slip of paper.

"In English, please, Markus," Mr. Waage chided.

Even though the phrase really means "here you go" in this context, Markus translated it literally. "Be so good, teacher."

Mr. Waage stared at him and eventually decided that the boy wasn't making fun of him, his English was just bad. "Let's see," he said slowly as he unfolded the crumpled piece of paper.

Everyone looked at him in anticipation, except for Sigmund, who had sunken lower over his desk, despondent.

"'You're still my best friend!'" Mr. Waage looked out at the class with a gleeful expression on his face. "Is this for me?"

Markus noticed that he felt a little warm. He felt his pulse pounding in his temples. "I think so," he said calmly. "But I didn't write it."

"You didn't?" said Mr. Waage, who seemed to be in a good mood. "Well then, I'd certainly like to know who my secret friend is."

Sigmund stood up slowly. "I wrote it, Mr. Waage. But I didn't write it for you. I wrote it for Markus."

"Ah, I see," Mr. Waage said, pretending he was disappointed. "So, Markus is your best friend?"

"Yes," Sigmund said calmly. "Markus is my best friend. And he will be for as long as I live."

"Well, well," Mr. Waage said amiably. "How nice that you boys are friends, but I would appreciate it if you guys kept that to yourselves until break. Now, Markus, can you give us some other English words for 'friends'?"

The pulse in his temples was pounding away like a machine gun. Somehow or other everything had gone wrong. No one was laughing. Everyone was just sitting there looking at him contemptuously, as if he was the one being a jerk, not Sigmund.

"Now, Markus."

"Huh?"

"'Friend.' English words. Let's hear them."

His head was completely empty. It was absolutely impossible to come up with any other words for "friend." Not in Norwegian, not in English. He stared out at the class, but there wasn't a soul who was going to help. Yes, one. Of course.

"'Pal,'" Sigmund said seriously and in English. "Markus is my pal."

"Very good, Sigmund," Mr. Waage said. "Any more?"

"'Buddy,'" Sigmund said. "Markus is my pal and my buddy."

"Yes," Mr. Waage said.

"'Colleague,'" Sigmund said.

"Yes."

"'Partner,' 'companion,' 'compadre.'"

"Excellent."

"'One person attached to another by intimate affection or esteem without sexual or familial ties,'" Sigmund said.

"Yes!" Mr. Waage yelled enthusiastically. "Perfect!"

"'Friend,'" Sigmund said quietly. "Markus is my best friend."

"And what a lucky guy he is to have you, too," Mr. Waage said, resting his hand on Markus's shoulder.

"OK, boys and girls. I want each of you to write me a little story about friendship."

Markus stared down at the floor as he walked back to his seat, knowing that not only Sigmund but the whole class was staring at him. The well-intended pressure of Mr. Waage's hand lingered on his shoulder. He sat down heavily. Then he raised his head and stared at the back in front of him. Sigmund was wearing the blue sweater Markus had given him for his birthday. He had the same sweater himself, and his old "pal" had said he thought it was extremely cool. No one else had a sweater in that exact shade of blue, and they wore them as often as they could, but today Markus was just wearing a shirt. A yellow shirt with an itchy collar. Markus thought Sigmund was about to turn around because surely he could tell that Markus was sitting behind him and staring. The blue sweater in front of him bent down over his desk. Sigmund had started to write "A Little Story About Friendship."

Markus opened his notebook. *I have no friends*, he wrote.

Class was almost over. Sigmund was still writing. At a furious pace.

Markus glanced down at his own story. *I have no friends. Have no friends. No friends. Friends.*

Well, it was a *short* story anyway. More of a poem in a way. A fairly short poem, perhaps, but a true poem. Still, he wasn't sure if Mr. Waage would like it. He was probably expecting something different. A nice story about friendship. Mr. Waage couldn't care less about the truth, as long as the lie was written in good English. It didn't matter. He wasn't sitting here to satisfy the teacher. He was sitting here because he had to, even though he'd much rather be skiing to the North Pole. Alone. He raised his hand.

"Yes, Markus?"

"I was wondering if I could change seats," Markus asked in Norwegian.

The back in front of him jumped, but Sigmund didn't turn around.

"Why?"

"Um, I don't know."

Mr. Waage looked a little irritated. "If you don't know why, then I think you'll be sticking with your current seat assignment." At this point Mr. Waage suddenly remembered he was supposed to be teaching an English class and repeated the last few words in English this time. "… your current seat assignment."

"I think …," Markus began.

"What do you think, Markus?" Mr. Waage asked, winking at Per Espen, who sat in the middle of the front row, right in front of the teacher's desk. "What do you think Markus thinks, Per Espen?"

"I don't know," Per Espen answered in Norwegian.

"What?" Mr. Waage prompted in English.

"Oh, uh, I don't know," Per Espen said in English.

"Good."

"I think my hearing is starting to go a little," Markus said.

Mr. Waage looked at him in astonishment. "What did you say?"

"What?" Markus asked.

"What did you say?" Mr. Waage asked again.

"I said 'what?'" Markus said.

"What?" Mr. Waage asked.

"Yes," Markus said.

Mr. Waage looked a little confused. "I heard you say 'what.' What I was asking about was what you said before you said 'what.'"

Markus wiped a little sweat off his forehead. "Excuse me," he said. "I can't hear that well."

"Oh," Mr. Waage said, concerned. "How long has this been going on?"

Markus wondered if he should say "what" another time, to emphasize the problem, but decided it would be best not to. Then Mr. Waage would think he'd gone totally deaf and send him straight to the doctor.

"Not that long," he mumbled. "It just sort of crept up on me lately."

"Have you been to the doctor?"

There it was anyway. Markus shook his head.

"Have you talked to your dad?"

"That isn't necessary. I have just a *little* trouble hearing."

"It's nothing to be embarrassed about, Markus."

"I'm not embarrassed."

"I know an ear specialist."

"What?"

"A doctor. Maybe he can fit you in for an appointment in the next couple of days."

"Phew!" Markus said. "It passed. Now I can hear totally normally again."

But there was no going back. Markus switched seats with Per Espen, who was happy to do it. There was a lot more freedom in the back of the classroom.

"Can you hear better up here?" Mr. Waage asked.

Markus nodded.

"Good. Then could you please read your story to the class?"

"What?"

Mr. Waage looked at him with concern. This was clearly more serious than he'd thought. "Can you still not hear what I'm saying?"

Markus popped up. "Yes, sure," he said. "I can hear just fine."

Mr. Waage smiled sympathetically. "Well, that's wonderful," he said. "Let's hear what you wrote, then."

Markus picked up his notebook. "I have no friends," he began.

It was a lonely day. No one sent him messages in Morse code during class, and no one debated anything with him during breaks. Sigmund had spent the day with Ellen Christine, who was stuck to him like a leech. Markus pretended he didn't see them, while at the same time trying to enjoy the unhappy looks the Glob of

Flesh kept sending him. When Reidar tried to tease him, Markus pretended he couldn't hear, while Anne Berit whispered angrily at Reidar that he ought to be ashamed of himself. She felt sorry for Markus. And Markus basically agreed. He smiled valiantly back at Anne Berit and thought that actually her voice was really pretty when she was whispering.

Now the bell had finally rung, marking the end of the last class. Markus walked across the schoolyard by himself and out through the gate.

"Markus."

It was Mona.

"What is it?"

"Don't be sad."

"Sad?"

"It'll pass. You guys will be friends again. Definitely." She smiled at him.

"What do you mean?" he asked quietly.

"You and Sigmund. And then you'll be able to hear normally again, right?" She smiled again. Her crooked front tooth was as white as snow.

CHAPTER 4 "Why didn't you tell me this before, Markus?"

Mons was looking at him unhappily. They were sitting at the dinner table eating blood pudding. It wasn't exactly Markus's favorite food, but it didn't matter what he ate today. It all would have tasted like blood pudding anyway.

"I just had a little congestion in my ear, Dad. That's the truth. I'm fine now."

"Well, Mr. Waage wasn't fine when he called. He said the problem was so serious that he had to move you to the front of the classroom. I got the sense that he thought I was a terrible father."

"What?"

Mons looked at him, concerned.

"No, I didn't mean 'what,'" Markus said quickly. "I heard what you said. That's totally the truth, Dad. I've never heard better in my whole life. I hear great," he added and took a bite of the blood pudding.

"Maybe he's right," Mons said gloomily. "Maybe I've turned into an eccentric old widower who only thinks about himself."

"You're not *that* old, Dad. You're not even fifty yet!"

"If your mother were alive, she'd have noticed your hearing loss a long time ago."

"There's nothing to notice!"

"Women take care of their kids, while we men just let things slide. I didn't even realize you had a hearing problem until some random teacher called me and told me. I'm not particularly proud of myself, Markus."

"I don't have a hearing problem! Mr. Waage misunderstood."

"You don't need to try to make me feel better, Markus. I'm really not the one we should be feeling sorry for."

Markus gave up. His father's problem wasn't that he didn't take care of his child but that he cared too much and didn't know what to do with all his caring. The only thing Markus could hope for now was that Mons would be so overwhelmed with self-reproach that he'd forget the whole ear thing. Unfortunately, that was just wishful thinking.

"But now things are going to change in this house," Mons said. "I … Mr. Waage made an appointment for you with the ear doctor this afternoon."

"What?"

"THIS AFTERNOON," Mons said, enunciating each sound.

Markus pushed his plate away. Now there was no way out. Mons was so overwhelmed by his own caring that it was impossible to escape. Maybe it was all the same anyway. Surely the doctor would determine that there wasn't anything wrong with his hearing, and then everything would be fine. Mons would be satisfied. Sure, Mr. Waage might be a little mad, but that would pass. And Markus would get back his old seat behind Sigmund. No, wait, that was exactly what he didn't want. He wanted to get away from that jerk with the fake sad looks and the blue sweater. After all, that was the whole point. That was the point to all this stuff that there wasn't any point to. He got up from the table.

"Thanks for dinner, Dad."

"Sure thing, son. Where's your hat?"

"My hat?"

"Yes, your cap," Mons said. "HAT!"

"I don't wear a hat in October, Dad."

"And that's my fault!" Mons said, exasperated. "If your mother were alive …"

"I'll go find it," Markus said quickly, running out into the hallway.

"Markus Simonsen," the woman who walked into the waiting room said.

Mons jumped up. "Here!"

"Right this way, Markus," the woman said, holding the door open for Mons, who walked into the doctor's office ahead of her.

Markus stayed sitting in the waiting room, listening to the voices coming from the office. First the woman said something, then Mons answered, then the woman laughed and came back out into the waiting room again.

"Well then, you must be Markus," she said.

Markus nodded. "Yeah, the other guy is my dad."

"I thought he was you. He was so eager."

"He's just a little nervous," Markus said.

The woman smiled at him. "That's not unusual. Fathers don't often come here with their kids. Usually it's the mothers."

"My mom is dead."

The woman looked a little embarrassed. "I'm sorry."

"It was a really long time ago," Markus said.

She held out her hand. "I'm Dr. Bye. Ellen Bye, but you can call me Ellen. So, you have a bit of a hearing problem?"

"No," Markus said, following Dr. Ellen Bye into her office.

Mons was sitting in a chair by the window. When they came in, he jumped up.

"Just sit," Ellen Bye said. "Unless you'd rather wait outside, that is."

Mons shook his head and said, "I'd prefer to stay here with Markus. If that's all right, Dr. Bye."

"Her name's Ellen," Markus said.

"What?" Mons asked.

Dr. Bye looked over at Mons. "I told Markus that he could call me Ellen. You're welcome to call me that, too, if you'd like."

"Oh," said Mons, stealing a glance at the device she was taking out of a cabinet. "What's that?"

"This is a device we use for examining patients' ears."

"Really?" Mons said, scratching his right ear.

"Don't worry, Markus. It won't hurt," Dr. Bye reassured.

"I know that," Markus said.

"I'm just going to shine some light into your ears to see how it looks in there."

"Exactly," Mons said, scratching his ear again. "You won't even feel it. It just tickles a little."

"Are you sure you don't want to wait outside?" Ellen Bye asked.

"No, I'll stay here with Markus," Mons said.

"As you like."

"I mean, I am his father."

"So I understand."

"He's a little anxious."

"I am not," Markus said.

"I didn't mean 'anxious' exactly," Mons said.

"I understand," Ellen Bye said.

"He's actually quite brave," Mons said.

"I am not," Markus said.

"I didn't mean 'brave' exactly," Mons said. "I just mean that he isn't scared."

"I understand," Ellen Bye said.

"Markus isn't just my son. He's also my best friend."

"That's nice to hear," Ellen Bye said, peering into one of Markus's ears.

"How does it look?" Mons asked.

"Just fine," Ellen Bye said. "Let's have a peek in the other one, too."

"Yes, I'm sure that would be best," Mons said. "How does it look in there, do you suppose?"

"Just fine here, too," Ellen Bye said.

"Yes," Mons said. "I figured as much. Markus washes his ears every day. We're very meticulous about that."

"Dirt in the ears doesn't necessarily have anything to do with cleanliness," Ellen Bye explained. "Lots of strange things can build up in there regardless of how much you wash."

"Yeah, that makes sense," Mons said. "What are we going to do now?"

"Now we'll do some hearing tests."

Markus passed them with flying colors. He heard high-pitched beeps, low buzzing, and all of the words Ellen Bye asked him to repeat. Even when Mons whispered "Kunnskapsforlaget's Conversational Lexicon" as softly as he could, Markus repeated it without any problem, and Ellen Bye said that if Markus had a hearing impairment, then there probably wasn't a single person in the world who could hear normally.

"That's what I told Dad, too," Markus said. "It was just a little congestion in my ear."

Mons, who was both relieved and tired after the exam, said he was happy about that and that, regardless, it was a relief to have it confirmed. "It's better to go to the doctor one too many times than one too few," he said, smiling at Ellen Bye. "Now we're on the safe side and don't need to worry anymore, do we, Markus?"

"No, Dad," Markus said. "Now we can relax."

"Yes," Mons said cheerfully. "Well, that was that then."

"Yes," said Ellen Bye. "That was it."

"Yes," said Mons. "I suppose we're done for today then."

Ellen Bye nodded. "Yes, unless there was anything else."

"No, I think that's it, Dr. Bye," Mons said, scratching his ear.

"Ellen?" Markus asked a little hesitantly.

"Yes, you can call me Ellen," she said pleasantly.

Mons paid and held out his hand. "Yes, this was a relief," he said. "Thank you so much ... Ellen."

"No problem. It is my job after all."

"It must be an interesting job. Being a doctor, I mean."

Ellen glanced over at Markus. Her face looked strangely cheerful. "Yes," she said. "You do get to meet some exciting people."

"Yes, I figure you must," Mons said, letting go of her hand.

She walked them to the door. "Just call if there's anything else," she said.

"I will," Mons said. "Good-bye, Ellen."

"Good-bye."

"His name is Mons," Markus said.

"I know that," Ellen said, closing the door behind them.

"There. You see, Markus? That wasn't so bad!"

They were walking down the tree-lined walkway from the doctor's office toward the parking lot. Mons was in a good mood, and Markus, who for a few hours had forgotten his broken heart and the friendship he'd lost, wasn't feeling so bad himself.

"No," he said. "It was just fine."

"Ellen is a good doctor, don't you think?"

"Yeah," Markus answered. "She's great."

"Did you notice her fingers?"

"No."

"She had incredibly long fingers. Really long fingers." He scratched his ear. "Do you know, Markus," he said, "I wonder if I don't need a little ear checkup myself. It feels exactly as if I have a bit of congestion in my right ear. Do you think it's dirt?"

"I don't know, Dad."

"Maybe I should ask Ellen to take a look at it."

"I think you should," Markus said. "It's better to go to the doctor one too many times than one too few."

"That's exactly what I think, too," Mons said and started whistling.

CHAPTER 5

Markus woke up in love with Mona. It happened while he was sleeping. She came to him in a dream with outstretched arms. "I'm the one you love," she'd said and smiled at him with that mouth full of pretty, white crooked teeth. A string of rough pearls behind red lips.

It was an amazing dream. A revelation. It was all clear to him. He had finally seen clearly in the dream. Her. The woman in his life. Mona.

He closed his eyes and tried to dream some more, but of course that didn't work. He heard Mons singing from the kitchen. "'Oh, what a beautiful morning.'" Markus hummed along from bed. It really was a lovely morning. Even the weather was nice. The sun was shining through the window. The wind was rustling in the trees. Two cats were howling in the distance. The air was full of love. So was he. Mona, Mona, Mona! Markus jumped out of bed. Off with his pajamas. On with his underwear. Socks. T-shirt. Hip, hip, hurrah! What a day! Oh, what a beautiful morning! Where are my pants? Where's my sweater? He stopped and stood there in the middle of the room with his pants in his hand. What would he say to Ellen Christine? After all, she thought he was in love with her. No, that's not true. She didn't think that. She was with Sigmund. Sigmund had understood that Markus's so-called love was just a dead end and bore the brunt of it himself. Said that he'd written that stupid essay about the ridiculous mermaid with the awful ears instead of Markus. Good old Sigmund. A true friend indeed. Faithful, loyal, and wise. And *he* had sold Sigmund out! But now he would make it right again. He would ask his best friend for forgiveness, move back to his old seat, send encouraging Morse code messages and exciting notes, and then he would be together with Mona.

He smiled happily and then felt how his smile hardened. The sense of happiness slowly faded away. That was only part of the dream. He hadn't been completely awake until now. The heavy thoughts of reality came back to him. Him together with Mona! What was he thinking? He was never going to be with anyone. He was never going to tell her he loved her. He was the most cowardly boy in the world. There was only one person who could help him now and he wasn't at all sure that Sigmund would accept an apology. A friend who has been disloyal once might be disloyal again. He'd dug a grave for his best friend and fallen into it himself. How could he be so stupid? He hadn't understood anything. Even when Sigmund had stood up in class and said, "Markus is my best friend." Markus had been blinded by jealousy and wounded pride and hadn't understood that Sigmund had saved him from a destiny worse than death.

Why did it have to be like this? Why did he always do the wrong things? Because he was who he was. Markus Simonsen! Not just the most cowardly but also the stupidest boy in the world. He put his pants on, walked over to the closet, and took out his blue sweater, even though he didn't think that would fix things. Mons was still singing, and Markus went to the kitchen to see if he could manage to eat a piece of bread with liverwurst.

•

Markus closed the front door behind him and went out onto the stairs. Then he opened it again, went in, and came out again. He did this three times. Not because he'd forgotten anything but because three was his lucky number. He had a faint hope that if he opened and closed the door, went out, and into the house three times, Sigmund would be waiting down at the intersection for him today, too. He walked cautiously down the road. When he tested it carefully, his ankle still hurt a little. Yesterday he'd only sprained it when he tripped. Today he'd probably break the whole leg. Markus had always thought that life gets worse and worse as time goes by. There was a boy standing at the intersection. A boy in brown velvet pants and a blue sweater. He was standing with his back to Markus and removing something or other from the sidewalk. Markus started running but stopped when the boy turned around. They looked at each other. They were about fifteen feet apart. Sigmund was holding a rock in his hand.

Markus tried to smile but wasn't quite sure if he pulled it off. "You have a rock in your hand," he said.

Sigmund threw the rock into the bushes next to the road. "Not anymore." He wasn't managing to smile either.

"Are you throwing rocks?" Markus asked.

"I'm cleaning them off the sidewalk," Sigmund said. The boy who could keep a conversation going was back!

"Oh," Markus replied.

"Someone might trip on them."

Markus worked on his smile. "So you're being a detective?"

"Yup. A crime scene investigator. How's it going with your ears?"

"Just fine. It was just a little congestion."

Sigmund nodded. "That's what I was assuming."

They stood there for a little while without saying anything.

"Sigmund?"

"Markus."

"I'm sorry," Markus said.

"No, I'm the one who messed up."

"No, it was me."

"Are we going to argue about *this*, too?"

Markus shook his head. "I don't want to argue. I'm sorry, Sigmund."

Sigmund picked up another rock from the sidewalk and tossed it into the bushes. "Me, too."

"It was my fault."

"No, it was mine."

"I'm a jerk."

"No, I'm the jerk."

"No, I am."

"No, Markus. The jerk is me."

Markus was starting to get a little irritated. Couldn't he even apologize now without Sigmund having to debate it?

"No, it's me," he said, losing his temper. "I ratted you out in front of the whole class."

"And I know why you did," Sigmund said. "I stole your girl."

"She isn't my girl!"

"No, but she will be soon."

"What?"

"I told her the truth yesterday afternoon."

"Oh no," Markus said.

"Oh yes," Sigmund said. "I said you were the one who wrote all those beautiful words and not me."

Markus felt the blood disappear from his head and collect down in his toes. "You said that?"

"I did, and then I said that you loved her."

Markus tried to swallow the lukewarm saliva that had collected in his mouth. "What did she say then?"

"She broke up with me, and now she wants to invite you instead."

"Invite me? Invite me where?"

"To her birthday party."

Markus felt his teeth start chattering in his mouth. "Why ... why ... does she want to invite me?"

"I assume it's because she's in love with you."

"She is not. She's in love with you!"

"Not anymore," Sigmund said with satisfaction. "I'm afraid she considers me just an unfortunate episode in her life. She thinks I'm a jerk, and I am, too. This is your opportunity, Markus. I envy you."

Markus had never been invited to any girl's birthday party before, but he had a real hunch that the time would mostly be devoted to small talk, telling secrets, and dancing. He'd only danced once in his life, and he'd sworn that that would be the last time. At Ellen Christine's party he was sure they'd start dancing the second they took their coats off, and when they were done, he was sure they'd turn the lights off. And he didn't even dare to imagine what would happen then, but even though he tried not to, he couldn't help imagining it. The thought of finding himself in a dark room with Ellen Christine's ear against his cheek filled him with an unspeakable terror.

"Damn," he said softly. "Damn, damn, damn."

Sigmund looked at him in surprise. "Is something wrong?"

"I don't want to go to Ellen Christine's party!"

"But you love her."

"No, I love Mona."

"But you said that you loved Ellen Christine."

"I was wrong. I thought you understood that … I thought that's why you …"

Sigmund shook his head. "I think we can learn something from this, both of us," he said slowly.

"Like what?"

"I'm not really exactly sure," Sigmund said after having contemplated it for a moment. "I see you're wearing the blue sweater."

"Yes, but Sigmund …"

"Does that mean that everything is all right?"

"No! Nothing is all right!"

Mona and Ellen Christine were walking toward them, a little farther down the path.

"Hi, Wormster," Ellen Christine called.

"Help me," Markus whispered. "What am I going to do?"

"Let's get out of here," Sigmund said, starting to run down a side street that led into the quarry where they'd built a lean-to when they were in the sixth grade. Markus followed him.

"Wait!" Ellen Christine yelled.

Markus pretended he didn't hear.

"He didn't hear you," Mona said.

"I know that," Ellen Christine said. "Poor Markus."

"Yeah," Mona said, "poor Markus."

They hadn't been to the lean-to for a long time, but it was still there. The heavy tarp they'd found in the stone quarry was still on the roof, and still hanging on the inside walls were some old pictures of the movie star Diana Mortensen, whom they'd both been in love with once a million or two years ago. Now they each took a seat on a wooden crate in front of the little table they'd fashioned. It was after nine, and they had Mr. Waage for the first two classes. Markus knew there'd be trouble, but that's just how it would have to be. He had bigger problems now than a teacher who took it as a personal affront when someone was late.

Sigmund looked like he was enjoying the situation. He was always in a good mood when he got to use his intelligence to help Markus out of difficult situations. "We have two problems," he said, taking a notebook and pencil out of his backpack.

"No," Markus said. "We have a whole heap."

Sigmund smiled at him pleasantly. "Let's start with the biggest ones." He tore a page out of the notebook and started jotting things down. "One: Wormster isn't in love with Ellen Christine and wonders how to say that without hurting her feelings."

"It doesn't matter that much if I hurt her," Markus said, agitated. "The problem is that I'm too chicken to say it."

"That's true," Sigmund said. "But the best thing would of course be for you to say it without hurting her. I mean, there's no way of knowing who you'll fall in love with next."

"What do you mean?"

"Nothing. It was just a thought."

"I'm never going to fall in love with Ellen Christine again, if that's what you're thinking," Markus said testily.

"Certainly not," Sigmund said, trying to mollify Markus. "I just think the most sensible thing would be to keep all doors open. Don't you agree with that?"

Markus didn't respond. It didn't matter what Sigmund wrote down as long as he helped Markus get away from Ellen Christine.

"Two," Sigmund said, continuing to write. "Wormster is in love with Mona and wonders how to tell her in a way that won't require him to make a commitment in case he falls in love with someone else."

"What do you mean about not making a commitment?" Markus yelped, overdoing it to beat Sigmund to the punch. "You mean that it's best to keep all doors open there, too?"

Sigmund nodded and said, "Yes. People should be careful to lock up after themselves, both the doors leading to love and the ones leading away from love."

He kept writing.

"What are you writing now?" Markus asked nervously.

"I'm just writing down what I said. I think it was really good." He looked up from the paper and stared contemplatively at Markus. "On the first point, it might not be such a bad idea to go to the party after all."

"Are you crazy?"

"Relax," Sigmund said. "It's a costume party."

"It doesn't matter what kind of party it is. I don't want to go!"

"You'll be wearing a mask. That'll make it much easier."

"What will it make much easier?"

"Saying that you aren't in love with her. It's incredible how much easier it is to talk when you're wearing a mask. It's just like playing a role."

Markus opened his mouth. Then he closed it again. It occurred to him that Sigmund might be right. If he was wearing a mask, she wouldn't see his face, and then it wouldn't matter if he blushed or stuttered. Maybe he could find a costume that would be natural to stutter in without making a fool of himself. An ugly costume that would keep people from wanting to dance with him or even a costume that would be impossible to dance in. That would make the whole thing much easier. He looked at Sigmund. "I'll do it if you come," he said.

Sigmund shook his head. "Unfortunately I can't. I wasn't invited. She hates me."

"Then I'm not going either."

"Wormster!"

Markus shook his head. "I'm not going to some costume party alone. No way!"

"Viggo was invited, too," Sigmund said, scratching his chin. "He's about the same height as me. He's saving money for a new bike. If we …"

Markus nodded enthusiastically. He realized his friend's brilliant mind was on overdrive.

"If we offered him twenty bucks, we might be able to convince him to let me go in his place."

"Yes," Markus said excitedly. "You'll be wearing a mask. No one will even notice the difference."

"No. Not if I don't say anything."

"You won't need to say anything. You could be ..."

"The Silent Knight," Sigmund said. "The Silent Knight never says a word."

"Great," Markus said. "Who should *I* be?"

Sigmund stood up. "Don't worry about it," he said. "I'll think of something."

CHAPTER 6 Mr. Waage had quite rightly been both angry and hurt when Markus and Sigmund walked into class halfway through the second hour, but Sigmund had explained that he'd been forced to accompany Markus to the emergency room because he had sprained his ankle on the way to school. Mr. Waage had accepted that because it didn't occur to him that his favorite student would lie and because Markus had limped into class in an extremely convincing manner. Besides, he was relieved to find out that there wasn't anything wrong with Markus's hearing after all. Fundamentally, Mr. Waage was a nice person, although he hid it well behind a bunch of sarcastic jokes that the students politely laughed at, but only Mr. Waage actually thought they were funny. Markus got his old seat back. Sigmund asked Mona to tell Ellen Christine that Markus would love to go to her birthday party. Viggo happily accepted the twenty bucks and promised not to tell anyone that he had handed his invitation over to Sigmund. He'd been invited to the party because Mona was interested in him, and since he'd just gotten together with Trine in class 7C, he was just as happy to get out of it. So basically everyone was satisfied aside from Per Espen, who had to move back to his seat up by the teacher's desk and spend his class hours right under Mr. Waage's watchful gaze.

On the way home from school Markus and Sigmund talked about who Markus should go as. There were only two days until the party, so they didn't have much time. Markus suggested Dracula, but Sigmund shook his head decisively and said, "Too interesting."

"What about Long John Silver from *Treasure Island*? He has only one leg."

"A pirate? Are you out of your mind, Wormster? Girls love pirates."

"The Phantom?"

"Quit messing around."

"What about the Phantom's best friend, Guran?"

"You can't dress up like Guran—he's black! They'll think you're a racist."

"What about Goofy from the Mickey Mouse cartoons?"

"Too silly. You don't want to make her laugh at you, Wormster. That would just trigger her maternal instincts, and that could be extremely dangerous. We have to find you something disgusting."

"I could dress up as blood pudding," Markus said grumpily. "That's the most disgusting thing I know of."

"I know!" Sigmund said.

"Yeah," Markus said, sighing. "I figured as much."

Thursday afternoon the two young, costume-clad men left Markus's house. In the doorway they ran into Mons, who was shocked.

"Good afternoon, Mr. Simonsen," the Silent Knight said politely. "We're on our way to a costume party."

"I can see that," Mons said, looking a little uncertainly at his son. "That's a funny costume, Markus. Who are you?"

"Uh-uh," Markus grunted, hobbling down the stairs.

"He's the Hunchback of Notre Dame, Mr. Simonsen," the Silent Knight said and followed Markus down the stairs.

Mons stood there for a second watching them, then he went into the house to make himself a nice soothing cup of tea.

"I can't!"

They were standing just outside Ellen Christine's house. The Silent Knight was about to ring the bell. Then he opened his visor, and Sigmund's encouraging smile appeared under the knight's black helmet. He'd wrapped himself in an elegant red cape, a short black velvet jacket, and a white cotton shirt that was open at the neck. Under that was a mesh sleeveless undershirt that clung to his body. He'd pulled a pair of brown leather boots over the black leggings, which were so tight that all the girls could see that the Silent Knight has a nice butt.

Sigmund was very satisfied with how he looked. Markus wasn't, even though he should have been. His costume was basically ideal for a guy who wanted to tell a girl that he wasn't in love with her without hurting her. He was wearing a dirty gray wig that looked like a hairball the neighbor's cat threw up. There was a little green hat on top of the hairball. One of his eyes was stuck shut with a dirty bandage that had been soaked in red paint. His face was covered with big red splotches. A couple of his front teeth were painted black, and he had a wadded-up handkerchief stuffed in one cheek.

The heavy gray coat was so dirty that not even Mons would wear it anymore. A big pillow was sewn into the inside of the back to create a hump. He wasn't wearing a shirt because Sigmund thought that some red splotches on his chest would get people talking. The coarse wadmal pants were way too big and were held up by a pair of leather suspenders that Aunt Esther had brought him back from Tyrol last summer. Even so, the seat of the trousers was hanging way down his thighs. He was wearing a rubber boot on one foot and a wool sock on the other. A bag of gravel inside the sock crunched unpleasantly as he limped along. Under his underwear was a whoopee cushion he'd bought at a gag store when he'd wanted to surprise Mons on his birthday.

"Relax," Sigmund said. "You look great. Just remember to grunt when you talk."

"Can't you do the talking?" Markus pleaded, trying to keep the wet handkerchief in place in his mouth.

"No, I can't. I'm the Silent Knight. If I talk, people will figure out who I am. They'll throw me out, and then you'll be all alone."

"I'm all alone anyway," Markus mumbled.

"No, you're not," Sigmund said. "I'm here."

He flipped his visor back down and rang the doorbell.

Ellen Christine opened the door. She was dressed as the Little Mermaid. A rather obvious sign of what she wanted. Mona was standing behind her, wearing a lot of makeup, a blond wig, and a low-cut black dress that revealed that her breasts were almost as nice as Madonna's.

None of them noticed Markus, who had hidden himself behind the Silent Knight's back. He was fairly short himself, and as the Hunchback of Notre Dame he was even shorter. Sigmund had told him to bend over and walk swaying side to side—with his arms hanging down like an ape.

"How cool!" Ellen Christine said, gazing at Sigmund admiringly. "Who are you?"

Markus stuck his head out from behind Sigmund's back. "The Silent Knight," he mumbled.

Mona jumped backward with a high-pitched shriek.

The Hunchback of Notre Dame swayed toward her, grunting shyly. "Actually, he's Viggo."

"Oh," Ellen Christine said softly, pulling back toward Mona, who was staring at Sigmund with a considerate expression on her beautiful Madonna face. "And who are you, then?"

"I'm the Hunchback of Notre Dame," Markus said.

"I could tell right away," Mona said, still looking at Sigmund. Now her eyes moved over to Markus and suddenly widened. "Oh, wow, what a great costume, Mark— I mean, Hunchback from …"

She wasn't able to say anything else before her voice turned into a kind of gurgle, and she turned around and ran into the living room. A second later, the faces of nine other girls appeared in the doorway. They quickly drew back, and Markus could hear from the cheerful voices that the party was well underway in there. He held out his hand toward Ellen Christine.

"Happy birthday," he grunted.

Ellen Christine took the present Markus gave her, then dropped it on the floor, staring at the palm of her hand. "What is *that*?"

"A book."

"I mean the brown gooey stuff on the paper."

"Oh, that. That's just some crap that the Hunchback of Notre Dame has on his hands," Markus said.

"Noooo!" the Little Mermaid screamed, running to the bathroom before Markus had a chance to explain that the crap was just shoe polish.

"Good," Sigmund whispered from behind his visor.

"We're going home now," Markus said. "I don't think she loves me anymore."

"Are you crazy?" Sigmund whispered. "She'll be over this first shock soon. You have to play your part until she's really turned off, and then come clean!"

"How do I do that?"

"You tell her you don't love her. That will make her happy."

Ellen Christine came out of the bathroom and accepted the present Sigmund handed her. She left the book from Markus lying on the floor.

"Come in," she said. "Everyone else is here. We're just about to eat." She smiled cautiously at Markus. "That's a nice costume," she said. "You almost fooled me."

"Uh-uh," the Hunchback of Notre Dame grunted, limping after her into the living room. The gravel in his sock crunched.

The table was set and there was cola and pizza. A murmur went through the room when Markus walked in. Some giggled and some clapped, but everyone stared. Almost all the girls in the class were there, but unfortunately only two boys—one Silent Knight and one grunting Hunchback of Notre Dame. In other words, they'd been invited to an all-girls' party, which was rather unusual. The only reason must be that Ellen Christine wanted to use this opportunity to show Markus her mermaid costume and at the same time give her best friend a chance to get Viggo's attention by dressing up as Madonna. Hmm, if only she'd known that the Silent Knight was someone completely different. Markus wondered for a second if he shouldn't tell Mona. Then she would be pretty pissed with Viggo for sending a stand-in, and while she was feeling that, maybe there would be a chance that she would notice *him*. As a matter of fact, she already had and he didn't want to give away Sigmund, who'd probably be thrown out if he did. So the Hunchback of Notre Dame ended up sitting all alone with a witch, a ballerina, a punk rocker, an Indian princess, three clowns, a naughty wood nymph, a belly dancer, Madonna, and the Little Mermaid.

He glanced over at Sigmund, who had already sat down next to Mona. She was singing something or other into his ear. It was probably "Don't Cry for Me, Argentina." The Silent Knight listened to the song without a word. He looked really cool, Markus thought as he took a seat in the unclaimed spot next to Ellen Christine. His whoopee cushion worked the way it was supposed to. Ellen Christine jumped up out of her chair. Two of the clowns whispered "ugh," the Silent Knight nodded in satisfaction, and the Hunchback of Notre Dame grunted. The party was off to a great start.

There are many ways to eat pizza. Some eat it with a knife and fork, some hold the slice delicately in a napkin, and some do it their own way. The Hunchback of Notre Dame had his own way of doing it. After the whoopee cushion worked so well, Markus believed that he was beginning to feel comfortable being in character. He figured the Hunchback wouldn't be used to eating pizza, so he really hammed it up. Both Ellen Christine and

Karianne, who was wearing a clown costume and sitting on the other side of him, had moved their chairs as far away as they could. Now he had plenty of room to play around. There were five large pizzas on the table. Two of them were within reach, a Hawaiian one and one with meatballs and tomato sauce. He tried to pick both of them up while squinting at them with the eye that wasn't stuck shut with the bandage. They were big and soft and were about to fall apart in his hands, but the Hunchback was quick as lightning. He flipped one upside down on top of the other, making a kind of double-decker pizza sandwich. Then he put his elbows on the table and took a bite. Four meatballs and two pieces of pineapple dropped onto the table. He crushed them with his elbows and grunted in satisfaction. He assumed no one had noticed this maneuver, but he didn't care. He was totally in character now.

It was unbelievable, all the things you could do with two whole pizzas, and his imagination knew no limits. His pizza sandwich was still rather unwieldy, but the Hunchback of Notre Dame knew what he was doing. He mashed his double-decker pie into a sort of clump and sunk his teeth into it. The combination of meatballs, cheese, tomato, ham, sauce, and pizza dough was pretty good. Tomato sauce poured out of the corners of his mouth; a clump of melted cheese got stuck on his nose. Let it stay there! There hadn't been much food up in the bell ringer's tower. Now it was time to chow down! The clump of cheese slowly slid down his nose. The Hunchback grunted in irritation. Was that all? No, he'd forgotten the meatballs and chunks of pineapple that were stuck to his elbows. He licked up the sticky pulp. Now he was thirsty. A bottle of brown liquid sat in front of him. Hmm, what was it?

Beer? The Hunchback liked beer. But what was that straw doing in the bottle? A few drops of the brown liquid were left in the straw. Must get rid of them! He pulled the straw out, aimed it at the Little Mermaid, who ducked, but too late. A few drops of cola hit her in the face. The Hunchback of Notre Dame laughed raucously, then stood up and sat down again. Fart, fart. He laughed even louder and leaned back in his chair while he dried his face on his coat sleeve and glanced around to see if anyone had noticed what he was doing. Most of them had. The ballerina and two of the clowns had left to go throw up. Seven other people were huddled together on the other side of the table. Madonna was clinging to the Silent Knight, who was sitting with his helmet held high and nodding encouragingly to the Hunchback of Notre Dame. The Little Mermaid was still sitting in her chair. Her face was ashen, and a couple of tears were running down her cheeks along with the drops of cola.

Markus started becoming himself again. Had he gone too far? After all, his intention wasn't to ruin the party. He just wanted her to dislike him a little. In a nice way. He leaned over toward her. "Sorry," he mumbled

Unfortunately, he burped at the same time. He hadn't intended to, but two large pizzas had been too much for Markus, even though it was exactly right for the Hunchback of Notre Dame. He pulled back quickly. *Fthththth.* Wow, that whoopee cushion was incredibly effective! He glanced over at Sigmund. The Silent Knight had reassuringly rested his hand on Madonna's arm and probably wasn't paying attention to him anymore. Well, well. Sigmund was probably totally in character, too. A silent Knight has to be knightly; a grunting Hunchback has to be disgusting. That's the grim reality of life. But he wasn't the Hunchback of Notre Dame anymore. He was Markus Simonsen, and he was all alone.

"Thank you so much for the pizza," he mumbled. "It was really good."

No one responded. The clown and the ballerina came back from the bathroom. The naughty wood nymph and the belly dancer started clearing the table. The Little Mermaid dried the tears and cola off her cheeks. Madonna whispered something to the Silent Knight, who nodded. They got up and went out into the kitchen. When they came back, the Silent Knight was carrying an enormous birthday cake with the candles lit.

"There's cake, too?" Markus said as Mona started singing in Madonna's voice.

"Happy birthday to you."

Everyone joined in, and to his pleasure Markus noticed that the mood was beginning to pick up. Sigmund set the cake down in front of Ellen Christine, who tried to blow all the candles out at once. She almost made it, but one was still burning.

"I'll help," Markus offered politely. He got up, took a breath, and blew as hard as he could. The handkerchief he had in his mouth flew out and fell onto the burning candle with a wet *thunk*.

"I bet it's out now," Markus said, sitting down again.

Fart.

Mona walked over and turned on the CD player.

"You want to dance, Viggo?" she said.

The Silent Knight nodded.

•

The curtains were closed, and dim light from a red crepe-paper Chinese lantern made the room exciting and romantic. The punk rocker danced with the witch, the ballerina with the naughty wood nymph, the belly dancer with the Indian princess, two of the clowns with each other, the Little Mermaid with the third clown, and Madonna with the Silent Knight.

The only one not dancing was the Hunchback of Notre Dame. He sat in a corner and wondered why he actually existed. His wig was itching and the eye that was stuck shut was burning, but he sat completely still so he wouldn't fart. It seemed as if the others had forgotten he was there, but if he farted he'd probably be the center of attention again. He had no interest in being that. Madonna and the Silent Knight came dancing past him, and Sigmund whispered behind his visor, "It's time for you to make your move!"

No way. He'd already made enough moves as it was. The Hunchback of Notre Dame had done his part, and besides, Markus was sure the Hunchback wasn't a dancer. Oh no. He mostly sat around and moped while the others were sashaying around dancing. Markus felt a pang of tenderness for the Hunchback of Notre Dame. That guy certainly must've known some things about life. Just like he did. They weren't so different, the two of them. It wouldn't surprise him if he'd been the Hunchback of Notre Dame in a previous life. In a way he kind of still was. Markus Simonsen, the Hunchback of Ruudåsen, Norway. He leaned over with his head in his hands.

"Markus."

He looked up. It was Ellen Christine and she didn't look mad, just sad. As if she felt sorry for him. Every now and then his dad had that same look.

"Don't be sad. I'm not angry. Somehow it was just a little much."

"I wasn't really farting," he mumbled. "I've got a whoopee cushion in my pants."

She giggled and asked, "For real?"

"Yeah. And it's not actual crap on my hands either. Just shoe polish."

She giggled again and added, "I could tell. From the smell."

He scratched his head and explained, "It itches."

"You can take off the wig."

He shook his head. "No, then I wouldn't be the Hunchback of Notre Dame."

She smiled at him. "Well, you're not the Hunchback of Notre Dame. You're Wormster."

He nodded.

"It's not so easy being Wormster, is it?" she asked.

"No, it's not so easy."

"We could dance, if you want." She was giving him that pitying look again.

He stood up. The whoopee cushion made a faint squishing noise. He knew now was the time to make his move. Now or never. "I don't want to dance," he said. "I'm very sorry, Ellen Christine, but I'm not in love with you."

The sweat flooded his armpits. The gravel in his sock hurt. His scalp itched like crazy, but he was looking right at her with his open eye. She didn't look sad. Not at all. An expression of relief spread across her face. She smiled at him. He smiled back, and they stood like that for a second, face-to-face. The Little Mermaid and the Hunchback of Notre Dame. So different from each other and yet filled with that easygoing sense of camaraderie you often find in good friends, and much less often in couples who are in love.

"That's fine," Ellen Christine said. "I'm not in love with you either." She leaned over and kissed him quickly on the cheek.

He couldn't remember the last time he'd been so happy. "Sigmund!" he shouted. "Everything's all right!"

"Sigmund?" Mona yelped, letting go of the Silent Knight.

Someone turned off the music.

"Sigmund?"

A mumbling sound could be heard coming from inside the helmet. Mona tore it off his head.

Someone turned on more lights.

Sigmund looked as if he wasn't quite with it. He was sweating, and his dark hair was sticking to his scalp. "Hi, Mona," he said. "How's it going?"

She glared at him, then raised her hand and smacked him.

A red splotch spread across his cheek. He grinned idiotically. "Did I fool you?"

She slapped him again and ran to the bathroom. Sigmund stood where he was. He obviously didn't know what to do.

Then the Hunchback of Notre Dame made another move. He went over to the former Silent Knight and took him by the hand. "I think it's best if we go now," he said quietly.

Sigmund nodded, obediently following the Hunchback of Notre Dame as he limped out the door after having said a pleasant good-bye to Ellen Christine, who he wasn't in love with, but who was totally OK anyway.

CHAPTER 7 Sigmund was silent and brooding as they walked home from the successful costume party. When Markus thanked him for his help, Sigmund mumbled something or other about how horrible women were. Markus asked which woman he meant. Sigmund stopped and threw his helmet onto the sidewalk. He stomped it flat and said he was just talking about women in general. Then he started walking again, dragging his feet. Markus followed him. The red cape hung down over the gloomy knight's back like a dishrag, and the tight leggings made his butt bulge in a funny way. But Markus didn't laugh. He knew Sigmund was coming down with something, and sure enough the next day he wasn't in school.

They had P.E. first period, and the Nail took the whole class jogging. The Nail, whose real name was Jonas Fransen, had run the New York City Marathon and had come in number 4,114. He was a vegetarian, thin as a spaghetti noodle, and used every opportunity to work out. He ran to school, home from school, and during his P.E. classes. When they played handball, he was an active referee who ran back and forth at full speed, blowing his whistle nonstop. The Nail always smelled like sweat and usually sat by himself in the teachers' lounge. Still, he was always in a good mood. He was the teacher who'd accepted the smoking ban with the most enthusiasm. "A healthy soul in a healthy body. That's what it's all about," he'd told Mr. Waage, who smoked thirty cigarettes a day and didn't take such good care of his body.

Now the Nail was running along with short, rapid steps at the head of the class, leading them through the woods down toward Lake Ruud, where they were going to swim. He had a theory that cold water was healthier than warm water and that taking a dip in Norway in October would make their young bodies hardy. He himself never swam. He claimed he was self-cleaning. "My bodily fluids are my shower and my body heat is my towel," the Nail said.

Jogging with Mons had gotten Markus in shape enough that he was pretty much able to keep up with the others, even though he was definitely bringing up the rear along with Mona and Ellen Christine. Both girls were wearing Adidas tracksuits. Ellen Christine's was blue and Mona's was red. They were both quite stylish. Markus was wearing the gray sweats Mons had given him two years ago. The label said they were for sixteen-year-olds. "So you can grow into them," Mons had said, but Markus hadn't grown much in those two years.

He glanced over at Mona. She was running with long, even strides. Her strong chin and those big front teeth made Markus think of a thoroughbred horse. She avoided looking at him. The party had been a success when it came to Ellen Christine, but the road to Mona seemed longer than ever. The Hunchback of Notre Dame had made an impression that was hard to forget, but he was counting on Sigmund. He'd helped him once, and Markus was certain he'd do it again.

"What's wrong with Sigmund?" Ellen Christine asked.

"I don't know," Markus said. "He wasn't feeling that good last night."

"I'm sure he didn't dare come to school," Mona said. "He's afraid he'll get punched in the face."

"He didn't mean to trick you," Markus said. "He was doing it for me."

"He's an asshole," Mona said, running up the path away from them.

"I think she's in love," Ellen Christine said, winking at him.

It felt like his heart had skipped a beat. "With who?" he asked as casually as he could.

"Sigmund, of course."

Now his heart made up for the missed beat by beating twice as fast as before. "I thought she was in love with Viggo."

"That creep?"

"Yes."

"She definitely isn't. She hates him."

"Really," Markus said. "But then why do you think she's in love with Sigmund?"

It wasn't that easy to sound casual when his voice kept jumping into falsetto all the time.

"She thinks he came because of her."

"But I just told you guys he came because of me."

"Yeah, that's why she ran on ahead. It's not always that easy being a girl, Wormster."

"It's not always that easy being a boy, either," Markus mumbled.

Up ahead of them the Nail blew his whistle. "Pick up the pace back there!" he yelled. "Otherwise you won't make it to the water before it warms up again next spring!"

Markus was the last one into the water and the first one out. He dried himself off while watching the others splashing around and squealing and shrieking in the icy water. The last person out was Lise. She was the best swimmer in the class and very tan even though it was well into fall. It made sense that she dressed up as an Indian princess at the party, Markus thought, peering down at his own white body. There wasn't much Indian there.

Lise smiled at him. "You were so awesome as the Hunchback of Notre Dame," she said, looking as if she meant it.

"It was really easy," Markus said, pulling his sweater over his head so she couldn't tell that he was blushing.

Mons came home from work early. He complained that his ear was hurting and asked Markus if he thought he ought to call Ellen Bye and make an appointment.

"Yes," Markus said. "She's a great doctor."

"So you don't think she'll think I'm intruding?"

Markus looked at him in surprise. "Intruding how?"

Mons scratched his ear. "I mean, I'm not sure it's anything serious."

"It's better to go to the doctor one time too many than one time too few, Dad."

Mons nodded. "Hmm, you don't say. Well, when you put it that way ..." He went over to the phone.

Markus went out into the hallway and was about to leave when Mons came running after him. "I got an appointment this afternoon!" he said, agitated. "She said she could take me after office hours."

"Take you?"

"Examine me," Mons explained. "Where are you going?"

"To visit Sigmund. He's sick."

"Poor kid," Mons said, satisfied. "Well, I'd better go iron a shirt. Wouldn't want to look like a bum for the doctor, would I."

"No, you certainly wouldn't," Markus said.

Sigmund's father opened the door. Gudmund Vik was a university professor and almost as smart as his son. "I'm glad you came, Markus," he said. "Karin's a little worried, but I don't think it's anything other than a case of youthful melancholy. What do you think?"

"I don't know," Markus said, following Gudmund into the living room, where they found Sigmund's mother, Karin, who'd kept her maiden name and still went by Karin Bastiansen.

"He's been lying in his room all day, and he hasn't eaten anything," she said. "I'm going to make hot chocolate and some sandwiches for you guys. Maybe you can convince him to eat a little."

Sigmund was lying in bed reading a little book. When Markus came in, he set the book on his comforter and sighed.

"Hi," Markus said. "How's it going?"

"It is better to have loved and lost than never to have loved at all," Sigmund responded, smiling wanly.

"What did you say?"

"Not much. Those who feel great love say little," Sigmund said.

"What are you talking about?"

"I'm not the one talking." He passed Markus the little book.

"*Words about Love*. Why are you reading this?"

"I thought I might be able to find something comforting."

"Sigmund!"

"Yes."

"You're in love, too."

"How did you guess that?" Sigmund said in surprise.

"'Love and fear cannot be hidden,'" Markus said.

Sigmund nodded. "Ah, yes. That's a Ukrainian proverb."

"Who are *you* in love with?"

"Oh, just someone who can never be mine," Sigmund replied gloomily. "By the way, have you talked to Mona?"

"Yeah. She said you were an asshole."

Sigmund laughed hollowly.

"But Ellen Christine thinks Mona's in love with you."

Sigmund sputtered, "With me?"

"Yeah," Markus said. "Isn't that just typical? I was in love with Ellen Christine, then she fell in love with you and then you dumped her, but then I wasn't in love with her anymore, because I was in love with Mona, who's in love with you, but you're not in love with her."

It didn't seem like Sigmund had quite followed all that. "What did you say?" he asked absentmindedly.

"That I'm in love with Mona."

A twitch moved across Sigmund's face. "I know that. I mean before."

"Before what?"

"Before you said that you were ... in love with Mona."

Sigmund's words came out in short bursts, as if he were having a hard time speaking. It was obvious that Sigmund wasn't well.

"I said it was typical."

"What was?"

"That Mona was in love with you when I'm the one who's in love with her, not you."

"But why … why does Ellen Christine think that Mona is … in love with me?"

Markus glanced down at the book and read, "'If a woman loves a man, her eyes can't hide it.'"

"Old Norse poem," Sigmund said. He laid his head down on his pillow and closed his eyes.

Markus looked at him in concern and asked, "Are you really sick?"

"No, Markus. I'm not sick. I'm just lying here doing some thinking."

"Yeah, it won't be easy."

"No," Sigmund whispered. "Goodness knows it won't be easy."

"But I'm sure you'll manage," Markus said optimistically. "If there's anyone who can get her to fall in love with me, it's you."

Sigmund groaned.

Then Markus said, "But first we have to get her to fall out of love with you."

Sigmund didn't respond. His face was pale against his pillow, and he was breathing heavily.

Markus bent down toward him. "Don't be sad. I'm sure you'll be able to do it. You're my best friend!"

Then Sigmund opened his eyes and smiled at him. A dignified, heroic smile. "That I am, Markus," he said, his voice clear. "And I swear that I will never, ever betray your trust again!"

He got out of bed. He was holding his head high and wearing his purple silk pajamas as if they were a suit of armor.

Just then Sigmund's mom stuck her head in the doorway. She smiled in relief when she saw that Sigmund was standing up. "I was just wondering if you guys would like a little food?" she asked.

"Yes," Sigmund said. "We'd like to eat now, Mom."

"'Without food and drink even a hero is no good,'" Markus said, repeating a Norwegian proverb. He really wanted to seem dignified, too.

While Sigmund drank two mugs of hot chocolate and ate three grilled cheese sandwiches, Markus read the little book from cover to cover. He had no idea there were so many poetic sayings about love and wished he'd been the one to come up with them. He looked up from the desk and over at Sigmund, who was wiping his mouth. The only thing wrong with him was that he was way too good looking. Markus was convinced that girls almost always went for appearances. True, Ellen Christine was an exception to this, but he didn't suppose Mona would be. If she was in love with Sigmund, it wouldn't be easy to get her to change her mind. They'd have to find some way to make her think he was ugly, and that seemed totally impossible. Unless ...

"Sigmund, I have an idea."

"Let's hear it," Sigmund said pleasantly.

"What if you borrowed my costume?"

"What costume?"

"The Hunchback of Notre Dame. If you show up at school as the Hunchback of Notre Dame, I bet she'll stop being in love with you right away."

Sigmund stared at him in dismay. "No," he said. "We're going to do this my way."

When Markus got home, Mons was sitting in front of the fireplace in his bathrobe, playing the guitar.

"I was just sitting here playing a little guitar," he explained.

Markus nodded. Mons didn't get out the old guitar very often, and when he did Markus knew that it was either because he was sad or because he was happy. And he didn't look sad now.

"How did it go, Dad?"

"How did what go?"

"The doctor's appointment."

"It went fine. I just had a little too much earwax. Ellen irrigated my ears."

"Did it hurt?"

"Nope," Mons said. "It helped. I can hear a lot better now. But it could easily build back up again."

"Oh," Markus said. "That's dumb."

"Nah," Mons said, satisfied. "It doesn't matter. If it does, I'll just go in for a checkup. You don't mind if I play a little longer, do you, Markus?"

"Play as long as you want, Dad," Markus said. He sat down on the sofa and closed his eyes while Mons started singing, "'Oh my darling, oh my darling, oh my darling Clementine.'"

CHAPTER 8 "Hi there, boys," said Lise, passing Markus and Sigmund on her bike as they were walking through the school's front gate.

"Time to make my move," Sigmund said.

"Wait a little," Markus said.

He had the sense that something wasn't quite right but wasn't sure what it was. It was too late anyway. Sigmund was already heading over to Mona, who was locking up her bike. When he got to her, it looked as if she was planning to hit him again, but then she must have changed her mind and poked him instead and started laughing. Then he pointed at Lise. Mona stopped laughing. She looked down at her feet while Sigmund kept talking. Then she nodded and ran after Lise, who was on her way into the school building.

Sigmund walked back over to Markus. He didn't look particularly happy. "Now I've done it," he said.

"Done what?"

"Asked her if she would tell Lise that I'm in love."

"With who?"

"With Lise."

"Are you in love with Lise?"

"No, I certainly am not, but at least now I've hurt Mona's feelings. I acted like a jerk, and that was the only way."

"Oh no," Markus said. "But I'm in love with her!"

"I know," Sigmund said sadly. "That's why I said that *I* wasn't. I want you to know how hard that was for me."

"I don't mean with Mona," Markus said. "I mean with Lise."

"I don't think I can take any more right now," Sigmund said, walking away from him across the schoolyard.

Markus stood in front of the entrance to Mona's building. His friendship was depending on this. If he didn't tell the truth, he'd have to find himself a new best friend. Sigmund had stuck up for Markus a million times. It was his turn now to ask for a small favor. Small? What he was asking for was nothing less than the ultimate and absolute act of self-humiliation. How was *he* supposed to know that Sigmund was in love with Mona, even if Sigmund did think he'd been rather dense not to notice. "You're so self-absorbed that you don't even give a damn about other people's emotional lives!" he'd said. Markus had retorted that if there was anything he didn't give a damn about it was Sigmund's emotional life. He didn't even give a damn about his own stupid emotional life. There wasn't much there to brag about anyway. He'd hoped that would make his friend feel sorry for him. But no chance! Sigmund was ruthless. It was the truth and friendship or keep quiet and be friendless. Or as Sigmund put it: "To be friends or not to be friends. That is the question."

When he rang the doorbell, Ellen Christine opened the door. "Hi, Wormster," she said, surprised.

"Hi, Ellen Christine. Is that you?"

"No, I'm Mona wearing a costume."

"Oh, you are?"

"No, silly, I'm Ellen Christine."

"Oh, I thought you said …"

"I was just kidding," Ellen Christine said.

"I see," Markus said. "Where's Mona?"

"In her room."

"I have to talk to her."

"I don't know if that's such a good idea. She's very sad."

"I think she might be in a better mood once I've talked to her," Markus said and then cleared his throat.

Mona was sitting in front of the mirror in her room and putting on makeup when they walked in. She turned around, and Markus noticed that she had mascara on her cheeks and lipstick way outside her lips. It wasn't hard to tell that she'd been crying.

"Hi, Wormster," she said quietly. "Is that you?"

He wondered if he should say he was Sigmund wearing a costume but had a feeling she wouldn't find that particularly funny. "Yes," he said.

"He wants to talk to you," Ellen Christine said.

"Oh, he does, does he?" Mona said.

She turned back toward the mirror and rubbed the lipstick off her crooked front tooth. "Well, what does he want to talk to me about?"

"I don't know," Ellen Christine said, sitting down on the bed, "but he said that it would put you in a good mood."

"Yup," Markus said, trying to make his voice sound cheerful. "Your makeup is a little smudged, I notice."

Well, at least he was talking. That was something, anyway.

From the corner of his eye he saw Ellen Christine make a face at him. "But that doesn't matter," he said quickly. "Mine was smudged, too. When I was the Hunchback of Notre Dame. Not that *you* look like the Hunchback of Notre Dame. That would be a sight to see!"

He laughed cheerfully at his own joke. This is how frogs laugh, he thought. It was unbelievable how good he was at finding the right words. He was on a roll now! "Oh no," he continued in a high, shrill voice.

"The Hunchback of Notre Dame is ugly and disgusting. He has red splotches on his face, a hump on his back, crooked front teeth and ..."

Bam!

Mona leaned her head against the mirror and sobbed as if her heart were breaking. Markus looked over at Ellen Christine for help, but she was hiding behind a magazine. He was totally alone in a girl's room with one girl who was bawling and one who was pretending he wasn't there. The walls were covered with pictures of Sting, Leonardo DiCaprio, the Spice Girls, Brad Pitt, Mel Gibson, and other celebrities he didn't recognize. He would've liked to be hanging up there, too, but the best he could hope for was a bathroom wall as the Hunchback of Notre Dame. The chances of that were good. Several of the girls had taken his picture at the costume party, and those pictures would certainly keep the memory alive for a lifetime.

He went over to Mona and put his hand carefully on her shoulder. She drooped a little, but he gulped three times and didn't pull his hand away. "I think your front teeth are really pretty, Mona," he whispered. "That's why I fell in love with you."

The magazine behind him rustled. Mona turned around and shot him a look that was simultaneously miserable and astounded. "You're in love with *me*?"

He nodded eagerly. "I … I mean, I …"

He stopped. Now he had to choose his words carefully. But which words should he actually choose? "I … uh … I … well …"

He always felt a little unsure when girls smiled at him. Usually they ended up laughing and that made him feel even smaller than he was. The smile Mona was giving him now was one of the most confusing ones he'd seen. It sort of only involved her mouth and made the expression in her eyes seem even sadder. Anyway, it was obvious that she wasn't going to laugh, but what was she going to do? Hit him, maybe. After all, she seemed to hit people fairly often. She took his hand. He closed his eyes and waited for the smack. It didn't come.

"Was that why you thought I'd be in a good mood, Markus?"

"Huh?"

Why wasn't she calling him Wormster? Usually she always called him Wormster. Now she placed her hand on his cheek. What was going on here? Sigmund! Help!

"It's OK by me."

"What is?" he croaked.

"I'd love to go out with you if you want."

Markus opened and shut his mouth three times. The Spice Girls peered cheerfully down at him from the wall, Mel Gibson smiled, Brad Pitt looked as if he wanted to fight, and Leonardo DiCaprio stared straight through him with a dreamy expression in his eyes. It was time to make his move. "No," he said. "I'm not in love with you. Sigmund is in love with you."

Then he explained everything.

Girls' emotional lives had always been a mystery to Markus. It was as if their hearts were always on a roller coaster. Up and down, from sorrow to joy and hate to love before you knew it. He could see from Mona's face that she ran through each of them as he explained.

Ellen Christine had gotten up from the bed. She was clearly excited. But not half as happy as her friend. Mona stood up and gave Markus an elated kiss on the cheek. "I love you, Wormster!" she said.

"Ugh!"

"Is it true?"

"Who would know better than you?" Markus asked anxiously, pulling away a little.

"I mean is it true that Sigmund is in love with me?"

"Yes," Markus said, relieved. "He's head over heels in love. On his knees, actually," he added to emphasize the severity.

"And what about his being in love with me, too?" Ellen Christine asked.

"Yes," Markus said. "That's why he didn't tell you I was the one who wrote the essay, but then he ended up saying it anyway because he didn't want to stand in my way."

"Poor Sigmund," Ellen Christine said.

"Yes," Markus said.

"He's wonderful," Mona said.

"Amazing," Ellen Christine said.

"The most wonderful guy in the world," Mona said.

"Yes," Markus said.

"He's so selfless," Ellen Christine said.

"Yeah, he really thinks about other people," Mona said.

"He has a heart of gold," Ellen Christine said.

"Yes," Markus said.

"I love him," Mona said.

"I can totally understand why," Ellen Christine said.

"Me, too," Markus said, glancing up at the picture of Leonardo DiCaprio. Then he opened his eyes wide and tried to look at the girls with the same dreamy expression as their hero on the wall.

"Is something wrong, Wormster?" Ellen Christine asked. "You look so weird."

"No, it's nothing," Markus said, rubbing his eyes. "I was just thinking about Sigmund. He's definitely amazing." He tried to do Mel Gibson's smile, but he didn't quite capture that one either.

"Do you know where he is, Wormster?" Mona asked. Now she was smiling with her whole face.

"Yes," Markus said. "He's sitting in the bushes outside, waiting. He wondered if you guys wanted to go to the movies."

It took a half hour for Mona to put on her makeup so that no one could tell she'd been crying. Markus was starting to worry that Sigmund would give up and go home, but he didn't. He was sitting behind a bush reading *Words about Love*, even though Markus was sure he must know it all by heart. When they came out, he leaped up and searched each of their faces uncertainly. Markus nodded to show that everything was all right, but by then

Mona had already run over to Sigmund and thrown her arms around him.

Girls and kissing are a curious thing. It's not easy to get them to kiss, but once they do, it's like they never stop. Mona and Sigmund took their time, and Markus was starting to wonder how long they could keep going before they ran out of air. He looked over at Ellen Christine and wondered if she was thinking the same thing. It didn't seem like she was. She was just standing there fingering her dress, then she looked over at Markus and smiled one of those peculiar girl smiles. He had an uncomfortable feeling that she was planning on doing a little kissing herself, to keep the other two company. He never found out because just then their mouths sprang apart with a little pop.

"Oh, Sigmund," Mona said.

"Oh, Mona," Sigmund said.

"Ahem," Markus said. "Should we go to the movies or what?"

They strolled down the road. Sigmund and Mona still had their arms around each other.

Markus and Ellen Christine were walking a little behind them. Ellen Christine looked a little sad, and Markus wasn't feeling all that great either, even though he should have been happy. Because now everything had all worked out.

"If I were you, I'd clean it off," Ellen Christine whispered.

"Clean what off?"

"The lipstick on your cheek. I don't think Sigmund will like it."

He rubbed at his cheek.

"Here, I'll do it," Ellen Christine said.

She took out a handkerchief and spit on it. Then she wiped Mona's lipstick off his cheek, and Markus thought that this was the closest he'd ever come to kissing a girl.

CHAPTER 9 They were going to see a movie called *Legends of the Fall*. Ellen Christine had already seen it four times and Mona three. *Legends of the Fall* was a movie about desire, jealousy, and death, all topics that Markus knew something about. The theater was full of teenagers, mostly girls. There were a few grown-ups there, too, mostly women in their forties and fifties. Brad Pitt was playing the lead role, Tristan. Markus had only ever seen him in magazines and on Mona's wall, but based on the reviews, he was kind of a stud. That certainly seemed true, because when he came riding across the movie screen, the girls in the room squealed so loudly that Markus almost felt as if he had water in his otherwise healthy ears.

They sat in the last row and Markus tried to share his chocolate-covered peanuts with the other three without rustling the bag. They were cheering, too, and Mona whispered to Sigmund, "Isn't he handsome?"

Markus thought that was a little weird, because she was in love with Sigmund, wasn't she, but now she was in love with Brad Pitt, too. He glanced over at Sigmund to see if he seemed sad, but it didn't seem like it. He had his arm around Mona and was pulling her closer to him in a protective way. He probably wanted to protect her from Brad Pitt, Markus thought, and put a chocolate-covered nut in Ellen Christine's hand. It didn't seem like she noticed, because she just closed her fist and stared at Brad Pitt while squealing. Markus wondered if he shouldn't open her hand and take the nut back before it turned into a sticky mess, but then she would probably think that he was putting the moves on her and then the day would be ruined.

Legends of the Fall was about three brothers. Samuel was the youngest and nicest. He died in the war early in the movie. Alfred was the eldest brother. He was the honorable one who became a member of the United States Congress. Tristan was the middle son. He was wild and crazy and got in a fight with a bear when he was a boy. There was a father, too, but no mother, because she couldn't handle living out in the wilderness and moved. Anthony Hopkins played the father. He had a stroke in the middle of the movie, but survived as an invalid. It was an awfully sad movie.

Markus started crying when Samuel died and kept crying until the movie was over. The girls were crying, too, but they were squealing with joy at the same time. Typical girls, Markus thought. You can never tell if they're happy or sad. Sigmund wasn't crying. He was just sitting there, calm and confident, with his arm around Mona.

When the movie was over, Markus tried to look as if he hadn't cried at all, while Mona and Ellen Christine pretended they'd cried even more than they had.

"Wasn't that wonderful?" Ellen Christine whispered.

Mona dried her tears melodramatically with the backs of her hands. "Yes," she sobbed. "Wasn't he handsome?"

Markus was starting to get a little tired of that word now. He hurried down the stairs ahead of the others, while Sigmund was analyzing the movie for the girls. "That was an interesting story.

Of course the most exciting character was Alfred. That was really the lead role, because his character evolved the most."

"But Tristan was the handsomest," Mona said.

"Look at Wormster," Ellen Christine said. "He walks just like Brad Pitt."

There was a crowd of girls outside. They were standing in small groups wrapped up in quiet, serious conversation. Many were crying. A little farther away a man was walking with his shoulders stooped.

"Look at that guy walking over there," Mona said. "Do you see who *he* looks like?"

"Yeah," Ellen Christine said. "He looks like Anthony Hopkins after he had the stroke."

"That isn't Anthony Hopkins!" Sigmund said. "That's …"

"Why don't we stop at McDonald's?" Markus interrupted.

They had just sat down when the door opened and Lise came in. She was holding hands with a massive ninth-grader. His name was Olav and he lifted weights down at Tormod's Gym.

"Hi," she said, peeking a little shyly over at Sigmund.

"Hi," he said, waving at her with the hand he was holding Mona's hand with.

"Hi," Olav said. "We were just at the movies."

"Us, too," Mona said, pulling Sigmund closer. "Isn't Brad Pitt handsome?"

"Totally handsome," Lise said, resting her head against Olav the ninth-grader's shoulder.

"Brad Pitt is a girly man!" Olav said.

"He's just jealous," Lise said.

"I totally understand," Sigmund said politely, pulling Mona closer to him to show Lise and Olav the ninth-grader that everything was fine. He had a girlfriend.

"Have you ever noticed that Wormster looks a little like Brad Pitt?" Ellen Christine asked.

"No," Lise said surprised. "Does he?"

Ellen Christine nodded and said, "Yeah, especially when he walks."

"Markus is a girly man, too, then," said Olav the ninth-grader.

Markus had taken a big bite of hamburger and didn't quite know how he was going to swallow it. "Alfred was the main character," he mumbled, "because his character evolved the most."

"He's a girly man, too, if you ask me," Olav the ninth-grader said, pulling Lise up to the counter with him.

Markus stood up and said, "I think I'll be going."

"But you haven't even finished your hamburger," Ellen Christine said.

"I'll take it to go," he said and then yawned. "I'm just so tired." He darted toward the door and heard Olav the ninth-grader's voice behind him say, "Goddamned chick flick, if you ask me!"

Mons was sitting on the sofa eating pizza.

"Hi, Markus. Where've you been?"

"At the movies."

"Really? Me, too. *Legends of the Fall.*"

"I know. We saw you."

"When?"

"When we came out. Mona thought you looked like Anthony Hopkins."

"She did?"

"Yeah. After he'd had the stroke."

Mons blushed a little. "I thought the movie was so beautiful," he said, "especially when Tristan came home and his father couldn't speak."

"Yeah," Markus said.

"Then he picked up his chalkboard and wrote 'AM HAPPY' on it. Truth be told, I cried a little at that, I did."

"I cried a little, too," Markus said.

"You didn't see Ellen, did you?"

"Which Ellen?"

"Ellen Bye," Mons said and took a piece of pizza, which he held out to Markus. "Would you like some?"

"No thanks. Was she supposed to be there?"

Mons took a bite out of the piece of pizza. "No, well, I don't know. She said something about maybe going to the movies today."

"Maybe she went to see a different movie instead."

"Do you think?"

"I have no idea," Markus said.

"Maybe you're right," Mons said contemplatively. "She really wanted to see this one. She thinks Brad Pitt is a good actor."

"He's a girly man, if you ask me," Markus said and went to his room.

•

The next day he didn't see Lise at all. That's probably why they crashed into each other in the hallway after third period.

"Sorry," he mumbled, wanting to keep going, but she grabbed his arm.

"Watch where you're going there, Wormster," she said, laughing. "You almost knocked me over."

"Hey!" It was Olav the ninth-grader. He came stomping over to them. "What are you two up to?"

"Nothing," Lise said innocently. "We were just standing here making out."

"Hey," Markus said, pulling back a step.

"You'd better not be making out with my girl," Olav the ninth-grader said.

"Uh," Markus said.

"Because I'll smear you into this wall."

"Can you even believe it's possible to be as jealous as he is?" Lise asked, winking at Markus.

"Uh, yeah," he answered, tearing himself loose and walking away as quickly as he could without running down the hall.

"Goddamned girly boy!" Olav the ninth-grader yelled.

Mona and Sigmund were as much in love as the day before. Markus hung out with them and Ellen Christine during breaks. She also felt a little excluded, but at least there were two of them, and they pretended not to notice.

"You guys look like an old married couple," Ellen Christine said, laughing.

"Way old," Markus said, and then he also laughed.

"Yeah, we feel as if we've been together for a hundred years, don't we, Mona?" Sigmund asked.

"Yeah, Siggybiggy," Mona said.

All four of them laughed.

Mona suggested that they play tennis that afternoon, but Markus said that he was planning to go home and chill out. He had a little bit of a headache that he really wanted to get rid of. Ellen Christine said she was planning to take it easy, too. Besides, three was a crowd. Sigmund shook his head sadly and said that then the old married couple would have to manage on their own as best they could. All four of them laughed again. It was pretty funny.

In the afternoon Mons went out. Markus did his homework and cleaned his room. He was vacuuming the living room when Mons came home.

"My word, Markus! Are you cleaning?" he gasped, astonished.

"I'm just vacuuming a little. I think it's time I start doing my share of the housework."

"Well, that's nice."

"It's only fair," Markus said calmly. "Did you have a nice walk, Dad?"

"I didn't go for a walk after all," Mons said, taking off his coat. "I went to the movies."

"What did you see?"

"*Legends of the Fall.*"

"But you saw that yesterday."

"I thought it was so good I wanted to see it again."

"Did you meet anyone you know?"

"No," Mons said. "I didn't meet anyone I know." He lay down on the sofa. "I think I'll just lie down here for a bit. If you don't mind."

"Go ahead, Dad," Markus said, tucking his dad's coat over him like a blanket.

"I'm going to keep vacuuming. If that won't bother you?"

"It won't bother me," Mons said, closing his eyes.

The doorbell rang. Markus turned off the vacuum cleaner, and Mons sat up on the sofa.

"Are you expecting guests, Markus?"

"No, Dad. Are you?"

Mons shook his head and both of them ran out into the hallway.

It was Sigmund, Ellen Christine, and Mona.

"Hi, Wormster," Sigmund said. "Good afternoon, Mr. Simonsen. We thought it was so boring just the two of us so we went over to see Ellen Christine."

"Hello, Mr. Simonsen," Mona said. "Then we thought it was boring to be three people, too, so we came over here to see you."

"To see me?" Mons said, surprised.

"No, Dad," Markus said. "I think she meant me."

"But we think it's very nice to see you, too, Mr. Simonsen," Ellen Christine said politely.

"Why is everyone calling me Mr. Simonsen?" Mons asked. "You guys can call me Mons."

"We'll remember that, Mons," Sigmund said. "We brought

some Chinese food. We thought we could have a little party."

"How nice," Mons said. "Come on in."

The girls helped Mons set the table while Sigmund told Markus that Mona had suggested that they start a club.

"What kind of club?" Markus asked, trying not to show how glad he was that they'd come over.

"A friendship club. For all genders."

Markus looked at him skeptically. "Is that even possible?"

"Obviously it's possible. Mona and I are a couple. Neither you nor Ellen Christine are dating anyone, but you're my best friend and Ellen Christine is Mona's best friend. If we four can't do it, no one can."

"A club?"

"Yeah. We could call it Four Good Friends."

"What about Two Friends and an Old Married Couple?" Markus asked, noting that to his own surprise he was starting to cheer up.

"Anything is possible," Sigmund said.

Right then Mons and the girls came in from the kitchen with the food.

"Well, I guess I'll go hang out in the other room," Mons said a little uncertainly. "Have a good time."

He walked slowly through the living room.

Ellen Christine was staring at his back. "Hey, that was your dad, Markus!" she said as he disappeared into his room.

Markus nodded. "Duh, I know that."

"I mean, he was the one at the theater who looked like Anthony Hopkins."

CHAPTER 10 Now they were four. Sigmund and Mona. Markus and Ellen Christine. Two of them were dating, but all four of them were friends. Even Sigmund, who didn't usually give in when they were discussing things, had gone along with the girls' suggestion to call their club the Four-Leaf Clovers without even grumbling. They went for walks on Sundays, played tennis on Thursdays, and held club meetings in the lean-to above the stone quarry every Friday, until it got so cold that they had to move them to Mona's house since she had the biggest bedroom.

Fall passed and then winter. Mons went for regular checkups with Ellen Bye. He was always in a good mood when he came home, but in a bad mood the next day because it was such a long time until he would go again. Mona and Sigmund still walked holding hands, but they didn't kiss as often as before, and Markus wondered if they weren't starting to become friends, too. The Four-Leaf Clovers helped each other with homework, passed notes to each other during class, and spent their breaks together. Markus had given up hope of ever having a girlfriend, but a club with good friends of all genders wasn't a bad replacement at all. Maybe he wasn't a nymphomaniac after all. Life was pretty good, and maybe it would've continued that way, if it weren't for what happened on April 14.

Suddenly she was just sitting there. At the empty desk in the very back, by the wall. She had dark, wavy hair. She wasn't fat or thin.

She didn't talk much, but when she said something, her voice was low, throaty, and slightly breathless, as if she had a secret. She didn't wear makeup. It would only detract from what was already perfect. She'd lived in Paris for three years, but now she'd moved here. She had one brown eye and one green one. Her name was Alexandra, and Markus thought she must be the meaning of life.

The day after Alexandra joined their class, the Four-Leaf Clovers were going to meet at Mona's house. Markus and Sigmund were walking down the road. They took their time, because Markus kept stopping again and again to pick coltsfoot flowers along the edge of the road. Sigmund tried to pretend he didn't notice, but he knew that something was seriously wrong, because he'd never seen Markus pick flowers before. Finally he couldn't take it anymore.

"Markus, why are you picking flowers?" he asked.

"Because they're so pretty," Markus said breathlessly and sniffed one of the flowers.

"I see. Do you mean that?" Sigmund said, astonished.

"Yes. And then they're so sort of delicate. But soon they'll wither away."

"Yes. They will," Sigmund said, not quite understanding what the problem with that was.

"Yes," Markus said. "First they're buds, then they open up in all their splendor, and then they wither," he explained.

Sigmund gave him a concerned look.

"Now they're gleaming like gold," Markus continued, "but soon this spring will be over and where will the flowers be then?"

"I'm not sure," Sigmund said slowly. "I've never given it much thought."

"No," Markus said. "Who has time to think about flowers?"

"You," Sigmund said.

"Yes," Markus said bitterly. "But I am but a passing flower in God's natural world myself."

Now Sigmund was starting to worry for real. "Wormster," he said.

"Yes?"

"You're pulling my leg, right?"

Markus shook his head and said, "Oh no. Who am I but that I should pull my best friend's leg?"

"Markus, You're not making sense. You're talking like a bad poem!"

Markus nodded sadly and said, "See? I can't even compose poetry. What am I worth?"

"You're in love again!"

Markus looked at him in surprise and asked, "How'd you know that?"

"No one with normal feelings says so much baloney all at the same time."

"I only said what I was thinking," Markus said.

"Don't do that," Sigmund said. "It doesn't help."

"It doesn't?"

"No, not if you're thinking like that."

Markus was obviously taken aback.

"That's absolutely the worst sentimental baloney I've heard in my whole life."

"But you have to at least admit that a bouquet of coltsfoot flowers looks like a crown of gold," Markus said meekly.

Sigmund shook his head. "Are things *so* bad?"

Markus didn't respond.

"It's Alexandra, isn't it?"

Markus didn't respond.

"Is it her hair?"

Markus didn't respond.

"Her voice?"

Markus didn't respond.

"Her eyes?"

Markus didn't respond. His eyes had a faraway, glassy look. If Sigmund hadn't known better he would have thought his friend had started drinking.

"Aha, it *is* her eyes," he said.

"It's everything!" Markus said hoarsely. "'All of the others are one. She is a thousand.'"

"Is that a quote by Gunnar Heiberg?" Sigmund guessed.

"No, Alexandra said it."

"Of course, I see. Forget her, Wormster."

"Ha!"

"I mean, you've been in love before."

"Ha! Ha!"

"You know it won't last long."

Then something in Markus snapped. He flung the flowers on the asphalt and stomped on them. Then he started talking a mile a minute, with tears streaming down his cheeks. The outburst caught Sigmund completely off guard. He wondered if he should call a doctor. It seemed as if Markus was falling apart.

"It won't last long?! Not this time! This time it'll never be over. In love? Oh no, I'm not in love! I don't know what I am! She's ... she's ... And what am I? Dirt, a hagfish, a beetle, a creepy crawly, a rat, a worm! And she ... I'm going crazy. I think of nothing but her. I see nothing but her. Her! Her! Her! She's ... she's ... she's ..."

"The most beautiful," Sigmund volunteered cautiously, but Markus didn't hear him. He was totally lost in his own world, and there wasn't room there for any prompting.

"She's *it*! It! It! I even love Mr. Waage!"

"Mr. Waage? But Wormster, he isn't ..."

"Her hands!" Markus shouted, while Sigmund glanced around to see if there was anyone nearby. Luckily there wasn't.

"Mr. Waage shook her hand. She shook his hand and now I love his hands, too. Mr. Waage's goddamned ugly, hairy hands! Oh, Sigmund. I think I'm going crazy!"

That was the first normal thing Markus had said in quite a while. Sigmund took hold of his arm to calm him down. Markus grabbed his hand and held on to it. "Did you shake her hand, too?"

"No, I suppose I didn't," Sigmund answered.

Markus looked at him in despair. "I don't know why I just keep crying and crying. Do you think it's stupid?" He was talking a little more calmly now. It seemed as if his meltdown was coming to an end.

"No, not at all," Sigmund said gently. "Sometimes it's nice to just have a good cry."

Markus looked at him appreciatively. "You're my friend. … You're my friend, Sigmund. You understand everything conceivable."

Sigmund looked as if he didn't quite know what to say. "Well …," he said.

"Yes, that's just who you are!" Markus dried his eyes. "You must understand exactly how I'm feeling!"

"Well, maybe not exactly," Sigmund said, "but at any rate I understand that you're in love."

Markus started crying again.

"Um, it hurts," Sigmund said.

"Yes," Markus sobbed. "It hurts so terribly, horribly much."

"I mean my hand hurts. You're totally squishing it."

Markus let go and dried his tears again. "Now I've made a fool of myself!"

Markus was himself again, and Sigmund breathed a sigh of relief. "I don't know exactly what just happened, but I understand that you have a little problem."

"Little?"

"Maybe big, then. But surely it was good to get that out of your system?"

"No, it was totally awful, Sigmund."

"Right …"

"Promise that you won't tell anyone that I … love her."

"Yeah, sure, of course. Are you nuts?"

"Not a living soul."

"No way."

"They'll just laugh at me."

"It would never occur to me to tell anyone. This is just between the two of us."

"Thank you."

"Don't mention it. I mean, I'm your friend."

"Hi, girls," Sigmund said. "Wormster is in love!"

Mona had just opened the door. Ellen Christine was standing a little behind her. Markus couldn't believe his own ears. "But, Sigmund," he whispered. "You promised that ..."

"You are?" Ellen Christine asked.

"With who?" Mona asked.

"No," Markus mumbled.

"With Alexandra," Sigmund said.

"Hey," Markus whispered, tugging on Sigmund's jacket, but Sigmund just kept going.

"But he doesn't think he has a chance."

"I think he does," Ellen Christine said.

"Me, too," Mona said. "Wormster is handsome if you just get to know him.

"Yeah," Sigmund said, "but he doesn't believe it. We have to help him."

Markus had actually decided to try to get a job on some ship and leave town, but Mona's and Ellen Christine's facial expressions made him change his mind. They weren't laughing. They just nodded and looked at him seriously, as if they understood how he was feeling. When it came to true love, maybe girls were smarter than boys, and besides, Mona and Ellen Christine were his friends. Maybe Sigmund did know what he was doing. If he'd said that he was going to tell them about Markus falling in love, Markus would have run away, but now he was glad they knew. If there was anyone who could help, it had to be Mona and Ellen Christine.

"Yes," Mona said.

"This is a case for the Four-Leaf Clovers club," Ellen Christine said.

The girls walked into Mona's room.

"Thanks," Markus whispered to Sigmund as they took off their coats.

"Oh," Sigmund said calmly. "It was nothing."

The Four-Leaf Clovers sat in a circle on the floor. For the first time since Alexandra joined their class, Markus felt relaxed. Sitting here with his good friends made him feel secure. He had a good time in Mona's room. He'd told the truth here about Sigmund's being in love and his own confused desires. After that day he always felt a sense of ease come over him when he came here. There was nothing dangerous in her room. Here he could be the little, confused guy that he was without anyone laughing. It was good to be here. They were all friends here. All genders. Plus, tonight he was the center of attention. Not the center of attention in a bad way, like when you get picked on, but a popular center of attention who everyone liked and wanted to help. Mona had closed the curtains and lit a candle.

"Why don't you just tell her you're in love?" Ellen Christine asked. "That would make me happy."

"No way," Markus said. "Not for a million dollars."

"I'll give you twenty bucks," Sigmund said.

"Me, too," Mona said.

"And me," Ellen Christine said.

"That's sixty dollars," Sigmund said. "That's worth considering."

"No," Markus said. "It is not. I don't even know her." He smiled bravely. "I'm just a fool."

Both Mona and Ellen Christine energetically shook their heads.

"You're not a fool," Ellen Christine said.

"You're the least foolish person I know," Mona said.

"You can be extremely cool, Wormster," Ellen Christine said. "For example, that time we saw *Legends of the Fall* and you were walking exactly like Brad Pitt."

"That's just because I was able to get into character as him," Markus said. "I did that when I was the Hunchback of Notre Dame, too, but I wasn't especially cool then."

"That's just because you got into character as the wrong person," Ellen Christine said. "I bet if you were the Silent Knight, all the girls in our class would have fallen in love with you."

"Only until I had to take my helmet off," Markus said. "Then they would've stopped being in love with me in a hurry."

"You don't know that," Mona said. "I thought you were gross for several days after you stopped being the Hunchback of Notre Dame. When I saw you, it was exactly like I was seeing him at the same time."

Sigmund got up. "I have an idea," he said.

Markus felt how the fear started creeping down his spine. "Yeah, I figured you would," he said.

CHAPTER 11 Sigmund went over to the counter. Mona and Ellen Christine followed just behind him. Markus went last.

"Hi," Sigmund said.

The elderly librarian looked at him a little uncertainly, then she lit up. "My word, aren't you the young man who borrowed *The Guide to Good Manners in the '90s* from me?"

"Yes," Sigmund said. "Both of the young men, actually."

Markus popped his head out from behind Ellen Christine. "Hi," he said and then disappeared behind her again.

"And what will it be this time?" the librarian said with a satisfied smile. It had been a long day, and people had been borrowing a lot of bad books.

"Today we're here about the art of love," Sigmund said politely.

Her smile vanished. The librarian glanced over at the girls. "Aren't you a little young?" she said pointedly.

"They're for him," Ellen Christine said, pulling Markus up to the counter.

"Hi," Markus said.

The librarian pursed her lips. "I see. And what type of amorous arts would you be interested in then, my boy?"

"Whichever kind," Markus mumbled, bending down to tie his shoelaces.

"He's interested in books about famous lovers," Sigmund said.

"He's already read *Words about Love,* and now he'd like to find out more."

"Yes, I'm sure he would," the librarian said gloomily. "But I doubt we have what you're looking for."

"Don't you have *Romeo and Juliet,* for example?" Sigmund asked.

She lit up again. "Oh! Is it literature you're looking for? I thought it might be something more sex-oriented."

"Oh no," Ellen Christine said.

"Absolutely not," Mona said.

"No," Sigmund said. "Classical love is what has captured his interest."

Markus smiled wanly. "Yup," he said bravely.

The librarian looked as if she wanted to give his cheek a pinch. "Yes, well then, we have quite a selection. Do you think he'd be interested in *The Sorrows of Young Werther* by Goethe?"

"You've hit the nail right on the head, ma'am," Sigmund said enthusiastically.

"Ah, I thought so," the librarian said, glancing over at Markus in delight. "And then we have a collection of short stories called *The World's Best Love Stories.* There are a lot of beautiful tales in that. Do you think he'd like that one?"

She was talking to Sigmund. Markus thought that was actually just fine.

"Yes," Sigmund said. "Beautiful is exactly what he's looking for."

The librarian couldn't fight the urge anymore. She leaned over and gave Markus's cheek a little pinch. "You certainly have an inquisitive little soul, don't you, my boy?"

"Yup," Markus said. "Do you have *Tarzan of the Apes?*"

Sigmund's plan was simple, brilliant, and gruesome. The simple part was that Markus would try to get Alexandra to fall in love with him by copying literary models. The brilliant part was that then he could forget about himself and concentrate on what he was copying. The gruesome part was that Markus was the one who had to do it. He quaked at the thought and couldn't think of anything less like himself than famous lovers. Sigmund explained to him that that was just because he didn't know them yet. He would get so into what he was reading that he would definitely become a great lover whether he wanted to or not.

The five books they ended up borrowing were *Romeo and Juliet* by William Shakespeare, *The Sorrows of Young Werther* by Johann Wolfgang von Goethe, *The World's Best Love Stories* as selected by Mogens Knudsen, *Tarzan of the Apes* by Edgar Rice Burroughs, and *Dracula* by Bram Stoker. Actually there had only been four, but Markus had insisted that they should get *Dracula*, too. "What if I get so excited that I bite her on the neck?" he explained. "Then it would be good to know how to bite." They divvied up the books. Sigmund took the love stories. Mona took *Romeo and Juliet*. Ellen Christine said she'd like to take a peek at *Dracula*. Markus took *The Sorrows of Young Werther* and *Tarzan of the Apes*. Before they went home, they agreed to meet at Mona's house the next day to, as Sigmund put it, swap literary experiences.

•

When Markus got home, Mons was sitting on the sofa playing the guitar. In a soft, rasping voice he was singing a Swedish song about a childhood home and some rustling birch trees. When Markus walked in, Mons just glanced over at him and kept singing. It wasn't hard to see that he was feeling blue. Markus sat down next to him, opened one of the books, and discovered to his horror that the librarian had given him some kind of old translation, written in a funny-looking font. This wasn't going to be easy. He flipped to a random page:

𝔍 watchèd Charlotte's eyes; they wandered from one to the other, but did not light on me! upon me! upon me! who stood there motionless, and saw nothing but her.

What was this? These feelings were so familiar to him. They were his own. The only difference between young Werther and young Simonsen was that Werther was at least trying to catch the eye of the girl he was in love with, while Markus hadn't even dared to do that. The only thing he could learn from this was that watching her wasn't going to help. She wouldn't even notice him anyway. He snapped the book shut with a bang.

Mons was done with his song about the birch trees. "What's that you're reading?"

Markus put *The Sorrows of Young Werther* by Johann Wolfgang von Goethe down on the coffee table. "Oh, it's just something I borrowed from the library, Dad," he said as nonchalantly as he could. "Were you able to get an appointment?"

Mons had said that he felt like it was time to get his ears checked again. He'd been hearing sort of a weird ringing noise. He shook his head and said, "No, Ellen is leaving tomorrow."

"Where's she going?"

"To the Canary Islands. With her husband." He played a sad chord on the guitar.

"I thought she was divorced," Markus said.

Mons played another chord. It was even sadder. "Nope, just separated. Now they're going to try to save their marriage. She's coming home in fourteen days." He stood up and said, "Well, I think I'm going to turn in for the night."

Markus didn't really know what to say. He resorted to one of Sigmund's sentences. "Me, too, Dad. Tomorrow is another day."

"Yup," Mons said. "I suppose it is."

It was past one o'clock when Markus got to page 166 in *Tarzan of the Apes*. The young, beautiful Jane Porter was attacked by the ape Terkoz, but luckily Tarzan got there in time. Markus was dead tired, but he couldn't put the book down now. Not before he found out what happened. He blinked his eyes a few times and read:

Against the long canines of the ape was pitted the thin blade of the man's knife.

Jane—her lithe, young form flattened against the trunk of a great tree, her hands tight pressed against her rising and falling bosom, and her eyes wide with mingled horror, fascination, fear, and admiration—watched the primordial ape battle with the primeval man for possession of a woman—for her.

When the long knife drank deep a dozen times of Terkoz's heart's blood, and the great carcass rolled lifeless upon the ground, it was a primeval woman who sprang forward with outstretched arms toward the primeval man who had fought for her and won her.

And Tarzan?

He did what no red-blooded man needs lessons in doing. He took his woman in his arms and smothered her upturned, panting lips with kisses.

For a moment Jane lay there with half-closed eyes. For a moment—for the first time in her young life—she knew the meaning of love.

Alexandra was squatting, pale and shaky, over by the wall. An enormous figure was standing in front of her. Markus thought at first it was Terkoz, but now he saw that it wasn't. There was no mistaking those hairy hands. It was Mr. Waage, who was standing there pounding on his chest and growling softly. Markus jumped out of bed. The time had come. The inevitable moment was here when it would finally be decided—who was the king of the apes, him or Mr. Waage.

"Hey you!" Markus said quietly.

Mr. Waage spun around. His eyes rolled so that the pupils disappeared and only the whites were showing.

"Grmlffgrrr!" Mr. Waage snarled.

"Yes," Markus said calmly. Then he tilted his head back and let out his tribe's eerie battle cry: "Ahhhhh … ahh … ah … ah … ah!!!"

"Markus! What is it?" Mons was standing in the doorway, staring at him in horror.

Markus was standing in the middle of his room. He'd taken off his pajama top and flexed what muscles he had. "Um, I … I was just …"

"Were you having a nightmare?"

"Yes … no, not really … I … I'm going back to bed, Dad."

Mons tucked the comforter around Markus and said, "You scared me."

"It wasn't anything serious," Markus said. "I was just dreaming that I was fighting Mr. Waage."

"Mr. Waage?"

"Yeah, I thought he was a giant ape."

Mons looked as if he wasn't quite sure what to think.

"His hands are so hairy," Markus explained.

Mons nodded. "I see," he said. He didn't look as if he did.

"I didn't mean to wake you, Dad."

"I wasn't sleeping." Mons smiled at him, and it was only now that Markus noticed that he looked as if he'd been crying.

"What were you doing then?" Markus asked.

"I was reading. *The Sorrows of Young Werther*. It's a beautiful story, Markus, but awfully sad."

"Yup, it's sad stuff, Dad," Markus said and fell asleep.

CHAPTER 12 When they met at Mona's house the next day, Ellen Christine said that there was absolutely nothing for Markus to glean from Bram Stoker's *Dracula*. Sigmund said he'd found a couple of short stories in *The World's Best Love Stories* that he wanted to take a closer look at. Mona had been so behind on her homework that she didn't have time to read *Romeo and Juliet* yet.

"So, that brings us to you, Wormster," Sigmund said. "Did you find out anything from *Young Werther*?"

"I didn't read it," Markus said. "I read *Tarzan of the Apes* instead."

"Did you find anything in there then?" Sigmund asked, interested.

"Nah. Tarzan gets together with Jane after he fights an ape."

Sigmund scratches his chin. "He did, huh? Can I see?"

"It's on page 166," Markus said, handing him the book.

Sigmund read the section out loud. "Interesting," he said.

"Yeah," Markus said. "But unfortunately we don't have an ape."

"No," Mona said, "but we have Buster."

Buster was her dog. He was a boxer. He looked a little scary, but he was as nice as a lamb and extremely bouncy. He would never bite, but he usually licked everyone he came in contact with and he drooled a lot.

"Of course," Sigmund said. "Buster is the answer."

"Cool," Ellen Christine said.

"What?" asked Markus, who didn't quite get what Buster had to do with anything.

"If Alexandra sees you fight Buster and win, she'll be totally impressed," Mona explained.

"Yeah, but Buster doesn't fight. He just plays," said Markus, who was starting to sense an unavoidable catastrophe looming.

"But Alexandra doesn't know that," Ellen Christine said.

"She has handball practice on Tuesdays," Mona said. "We can bring Buster and wait for her outside the gym. When she comes out, you'll happen to be walking by eating a hot dog, while we're hiding around the corner. When you wave the hot dog around, we'll let go of Buster."

"Well, that's all decided then," Sigmund said.

"No it's not!" Markus said.

Markus wasn't happy about it, but at least he'd gotten out of having to do it shirtless, like Sigmund had suggested. He walked slowly toward the entrance to the gym, taking a small bite out of the hot dog and bun he was holding. Buster was whimpering like a fiend around the corner of the building. Mona had let him smell the hot dog, and now he was pulling so hard on the leash that it took all three of them to hold him back.

The girls started coming out after their handball practice. Markus didn't feel much like Tarzan and wondered if he'd manage to eat the whole hot dog before they released Buster. After all, he could just apologize and say he got carried away because he was hungry and hot dogs were his favorite food. He was just about to take a bite when he felt his legs go soft and warm, like freshly boiled hot dogs. There she was. Standing on the steps in front of the door. Not more than seven or eight yards away from him. In a white tracksuit with a face that was golden in the evening sunlight. He'd put the hot dog in his mouth but hadn't managed to either take a bite from it or take it out again. His mouth was paralyzed. His hands, too. Now she was looking at him, and it was as if the whole world was glittering before his eyes.

Then Buster came. Full speed ahead while barking loudly and excitedly, with his little tail stump spinning like a propeller. The next second, he jumped up with his front paws on Markus's chest, his mouth open and drooling, moving toward the hot dog that was hanging from the Ape King's mouth. Markus didn't quite get what was happening, but he had a faint sense that the dog was kissing him.

Buster ate his way up the hot dog to where it disappeared and somehow or other managed to suck the rest of it out of Markus's mouth. A second later, they were lying on the ground, entangled. They rolled around while Buster barked excitedly and searched Markus's mouth for more hot dog. Markus fought desperately to get free from the happy, drooling beast that was lying on top of him. There was absolutely no need to pretend he was fighting. He managed to flip Buster over onto his back. The dog howled excitedly, flailing his legs. One of his front paws hit Markus in the nose, so Markus howled, too, and a second later Buster was on top of him again licking every inch of Markus's face, searching for more hot dog. Then they rolled over again, and Markus was on top now. They were both breathing heavily. Buster licked his lips with his long, pink tongue, raising his head up toward Markus, ready for more kissing.

Markus threw his head to the side and they kept rolling toward the steps, barking and screaming. They lay there groaning, Markus underneath. Clearly Buster had decided that enough was enough. He gave Markus one last lick in the ear and trotted happily back over to Mona, who was waiting with the others around the corner of the building.

Markus got up and dried off his face. Now was when he was supposed to let out the victory cry of the Apes, but he figured he might as well just skip that. During the melee, he hadn't heard anything besides his own shrieks and Buster's barking, but now he heard some cheerful noises. He tried to look up toward the door but couldn't see. There were four girls standing on the steps. They were staring at him and howling with laughter. None of them was Alexandra.

"Her mother came and picked her up while you were struggling," Sigmund explained. "But I think she saw you," he said supportively.

"I think they both saw you," Mona said.

They walked down the road toward the subdivision. Buster had totally lost interest in Markus. It was fun while it lasted, but now he was off sniffing for a place to pee.

Markus didn't say anything. There was a tear in his shirt, and he was bleeding from a scratch on his nose.

Ellen Christine handed him a tissue. "That was quite a fight," she said. "Who won?"

"I think it was Buster," Mona said. "But it was close."

"Yeah," Sigmund said. "What do we do now?"

"Now we go home," Markus said.

When Mons asked why he looked the way he did, Markus responded bitterly that he was just fighting with someone bigger than him.

"How did it go for the other guy, then?" Mons asked, alarmed.

"He hightailed it out of there to pee," Markus said.

Mons, who'd never been in a fight with anyone, gave his son a look of admiration. "Really? You don't say," he said. "Well, I presume you're not the kind of guy who lets himself be walked all over."

The next morning, Markus went to the library and returned *Tarzan of the Apes*. Sigmund, who had waited for him at the intersection in vain, slipped him a note during first period: SUMMARY AT BREAK.

Markus passed a note back: FORGET IT.

He couldn't help himself. He *had* to look over at Alexandra. She was concentrating on her math problems and didn't see him. It didn't seem like the fight with Buster had made much of an impression. No, no. So now there wasn't any difference between him and young Werther. She didn't notice him, whether he was fighting or looking. He was invisible.

A new note arrived from Sigmund: IN THE BIKE SHED. BE THERE.

•

"It was the tail that ruined it," Sigmund explained.

The Four-Leaf Clovers were standing in the bike shed, going over yesterday's events. Which is to say that Sigmund was going over the events, assisted by Mona and Ellen Christine. Markus didn't say much.

"If Buster hadn't been wagging his tail, it would've looked like a real fight," Sigmund continued.

"I didn't think anyone would notice that since he has such a short tail," Mona said.

"Well, they certainly did," Ellen Christine said. "I've never seen such a short tail wag so much. Maybe we should get a different dog."

Markus shook his head.

"I agree with Markus," Sigmund said. "We have to come up with something else. I have a plan."

"I don't want to hear it," Markus said.

"But Wormster, come on," Ellen Christine said. "What if it's a good plan?"

"I don't give a shit," Markus said. "I have to go to the bathroom." He walked away.

"Poor Markus," Mona said.

"Don't worry," Sigmund said. "I know him. He doesn't give up that easily."

"What's your plan?" Ellen Christine asked.

"Well, I'll tell you," Sigmund said.

It was five thirty in the evening when the phone rang. Mons answered it. "This is Mons. Who? Oh, is it really you? This is really … a … surprise. …"

Markus, who was sitting on the sofa reading about the sorrows of young Werther, looked up from his book. Mons had started fiddling with his tie, as if the person on the phone could see whether it was tied properly or not.

"Oh, you're home already? But why … Oh, it didn't go well? I'm sorry to hear that." His voice was sad, but his mouth was smiling a weird, silly looking smile. "If I was free to … tomorrow … Wait a sec, I'll just check my schedule." He set down the phone and tied his tie, then picked the phone back up. "Yeah, that would work fine. Right, I'll see you then. I'm looking forward … I mean … it will be nice to get them checked. There's a ringing noise. Yes, thank you so much. All right, then. Good-bye."

He hung the phone up. "Ellen's back," he said, excited.

"I thought she was going to be gone for fourteen days," Markus said.

"Yeah, but now she's back," Mons explained.

"Why?"

"It didn't go well."

"What didn't?"

"Things with her husband." Mons trotted around the room. "I suspected as much," he said. "I suspected this!"

He pulled out his guitar and started playing. "'Oh my darling, oh my darling, oh my darling Clementine.'"

"You play the guitar, too, Mr. Simonsen?" Sigmund had walked into the living room along with Mona and Ellen Christine.

"We rang the bell," he said, "but it didn't seem like anyone heard us, so we let ourselves in."

Mons had stopped playing.

"You should really sing more," Mona said.

"That was really good," Ellen Christine said.

"It was, indeed, Mr. Simonsen," Sigmund said jovially. "We really like music and folk songs."

"Call me Mons," Mons said and walked into his room where he continued singing.

"OK, listen up," Sigmund said.

"I don't want to," Markus said.

"Mona and Ellen Christine have made friends with Alexandra."

"What?"

"We made friends with Alexandra," Mona explained. "Does he sing a lot?"

"Who?"

"Your dad."

"No, just sometimes. What did you say before that?"

"Let's start from the beginning," Sigmund said slowly. "One: Mona and Ellen Christine have made friends with Alexandra. Two: they know a lot about her now. Three: they will tell you everything they know. Four: that was my plan."

"Oh," Markus said.

"Aren't you interested anymore?" Ellen Christine asked. "You haven't fallen in love with someone else, have you?"

"I'll never fall in love with anyone else!"

"Good," Sigmund said. "Tell him, girls."

"She's really nice," Mona said. "And she thought Buster was really cute."

"Her dad's a diplomat," Ellen Christine said. "That's why they lived in Paris, but now her parents are divorced and her mother got a job here at a local radio station."

"Yeah," Mona said. "She's actually an actress. The mother, that is, but it's not that easy to get a job when you've been away for so long. But she's thinking about starting a theater group here."

"The mother, that is," Ellen Christine said.

Mona nodded. "Alexandra has been in plays, too. At school in Paris."

Ellen Christine nodded. "She's interested in lots of things. Handball, for example, and orienteering."

"What kind of orienteering?" Markus asked.

"You know, orienteering. It's a sport. Where you get a map and a compass and run a cross-country race going through the woods from checkpoint to checkpoint."

Markus nodded. "Oh, right. That kind of orienteering."

"What about boys?" Sigmund asked, nodding his head toward Markus. "Are boys also one of her interests?"

"No," Ellen Christine said. "She's never had a boyfriend. She says they avoid her. She thinks it's because she's so ugly."

"That's not why," Markus said. "It's because she's so beautiful."

"That's what we said, too," Mona said. "But she thinks she's ugly because her eyes are different colors."

"She said that?!" Markus almost yelled.

To think that anyone could bring themselves to say that Alexandra's eyes were ugly! It just won't do! Markus thought. The person who said that can kiss my ... Then he realized that she said it herself and he calmed down a little. "They're not ugly. They're beautiful," he said meekly.

"All right," Sigmund said. "So we know quite a bit, and the most important thing we know is that our dear Alexandra ..."

"What do you mean by 'our dear Alexandra'?" Markus asked, suspicious.

"Yeah, what do you actually mean by that?" Mona asked.

"Relax," Sigmund said. "I just mean that we know a lot about her now. We know she's nice, likes acting, animals, and orienteering, but most of all we know that she doesn't have a boyfriend and that she has no self-confidence. That simplifies the issue."

"What issue?" asked Markus, who had a feeling that Sigmund was well on his way toward his next plan.

"The issue we are working on a solution for," Sigmund said. "The issue of getting Alexandra to be interested in you. I think we can forget about Tarzan."

"I think we can forget the whole issue," Markus said.

Sigmund pretended he hadn't heard. "We've been attacking the problem from the wrong end," he said. "We've been trying to get Alexandra interested in Markus."

"But wasn't that the whole point?" Mona asked, surprised.

"The point," Sigmund said patronizingly, "is that that is doomed to fail."

Markus nodded gloomily.

Sigmund smiled at him. An infuriating smile. "Relax, buddy," he said. "Alexandra's problem is not that she's not interested in you, but that she thinks she's ugly and that you could never be interested in her. That means that ..."

"… that we have to get her to realize that Wormster is interested in her," Ellen Christine said.

"… because then there's a good chance that she'll get interested in Wormster, too," Mona said.

"Yes!" Sigmund said.

"No," Markus said.

"I brought *The World's Best Love Stories*," Sigmund said. "There's a short story in here called 'The Art of Love.' It's by Giovanni Fiorentino, and it's about how a master teaches a young man named Bucciuolo how to fall in love and what to do once you have. He gives him several assignments. The first is to find someone he's in love with. And of course, Wormster has already done that, so we can skip ahead to number two."

He opened the book. They heard Mons's voice from the room next door. "'Oh my darling, oh my darling, oh my darling Clementine.'"

"Funny song," Sigmund said and started reading.

CHAPTER 13 Markus walked by the house Alexandra lived in and looked up at the window. That was the master's second assignment for Bucciuolo:

"'You must stroll, respectably and calmly, past her window two or three times a day. But be careful that no one notices that you are checking on her! All the same, you must appreciate the sight of her long enough that she understands that you're interested in her.'"

Markus had already walked by the house four times, and he had the definite sense that he'd been noticed. She looked out the window every now and then, but drew back every time he looked at her. When he reported this to the others, who were waiting at Mona's house, both girls said that was a clear sign that she was starting to be interested. So now he was walking by for the fifth time. It was starting to get dark and he was cold, but he kept looking anyway. He thought he was starting to get the hang of this now and was even able to manage a sort of stiff smile. There she came, undoubtedly to look at him again. He smiled with all his might. A woman opened the window and he felt the smile get stuck on his face.

"Hello, there!" the woman hollered. "What are you doing sneaking around out there?"

Markus smiled but didn't say anything.

"If you don't quit skulking around out there, I'm going to call the police!"

Alexandra's face popped up behind the woman's.

"Thanks for a lovely evening," Markus said politely and ran away.

"How did it go?" Mona asked breathlessly when he joined the rest of the Four-Leaf Clovers, panting. "Did you make contact?"

"Yes," Markus said. "With her mother."

"Well, that's not bad," Ellen Christine said.

Sigmund picked up the book and read through it, then said, "Excellent. I'm very pleased with you; so far you've done great. Now you have to send one of those women who sell lace and handbags over to her house. You have her explain that you're at Alexandra's service, that there's no one in the whole world you love more than her, that you will do everything she wants. Once you hear Alexandra's response, come back and tell me. Then I'll tell you what to do next."

"Bye," Markus said and went home.

He was met in the doorway by an excited Mons. "Markus. There's something I have to tell you. I went to see Ellen."

"Do you need a hearing aid, Dad?"

"No, no, but … Markus … I mean, well, you don't mind, do you, if I … Well, you know what I mean."

"Um, not exactly."

Mons cleared his throat and said, "Yes, well. It's just that I … well, I invited her to dinner on Saturday if that's all right with you."

"Sure it is, Dad. Where are you going to go? To L'Étoile?"

Mons smiled, relieved. "No, I actually invited her over here. I thought I would let her taste my steak."

"What steak?"

"The steak I'm planning on grilling for her. Maybe a little red wine, too. What do you think?"

"That sounds sensible," Markus said.

"Oh, son," Mons said, hugging him. "I love you so much."

"Save a little of the hugging for Ellen," Markus said. He thought that was quite a clever thing to have said.

Markus was in the check-out line at Rema. There were four people ahead of him. One of them was a woman who looked like she was stocking up on everything she would need for the rest of the year. Markus had only a liter of milk. He had to go to the bathroom but didn't dare ask the woman if she would let him cut in front of her. She would probably just think he was being rude. That's what grown-ups usually thought when children asked to go first. He thought about it a little and wondered when he would be old enough to ask. Probably not for a while. Behind him, he felt someone pushing ahead in the line but pretended he didn't notice. There was no way he was going to give up his spot in line either. Even if the person pushing their way ahead was over eighty years old.

"Excuse me," said a deep girl's voice behind him.

He spun around and looked right into one brown eye and one green eye.

"Is that you?" Alexandra asked quietly.

"Yes," Markus said, even more quietly.

The line clustered in around them. It really wasn't easy to breathe.

"I wondered if I could just squeeze by you?" Alexandra asked.

Markus nodded in silence, and she squeezed her way around him while she whispered: "I don't need any lace."

Markus nodded again. That was obvious. She was in the grocery store buying salt. Who wears lace to the grocery store?!

The woman with all the groceries turned around. "Did you find the salt?"

"Yeah, Mom," Alexandra said, putting the salt in the cart while she looked at Markus with a strange, hurt look.

Now the woman was looking at him, too. "Haven't I seen you before?" she asked.

"I forgot the oranges," Markus said.

He turned around and got out of line. When he came back, Alexandra and her mother had left and the line was twice as long.

"It didn't say for you guys to give her lace," Sigmund said. "It said that you should get someone who makes lace and handbags to tell her that Markus loves her."

It was Friday afternoon. The Four-Leaf Clovers were walking down the path to Lake Ruud to go swimming. Sigmund was annoyed, the girls were embarrassed, and Markus didn't quite get what had happened.

"We thought we were supposed to give her some lace first," Mona said.

"You gave her *lace*?" Markus asked.

"Yeah," Ellen Christine said. "We told her it was from you."

"Huh?"

"It was just an *old* lace doily," Ellen Christine said, as if that made it any better.

"But then you did tell her that he loved her, right?" Sigmund asked.

"Um, no," Mona said. "We didn't get that far. Because she left. We haven't seen her since then."

Markus was still pretty confused. "Why did she leave once she got the lace?"

"Well, first she gave us back the lace," Ellen Christine explained.

"Why?"

"I guess she thought you were making fun of her."

"That I was …?"

"Yeaaaaah," Mona said. "She said that we should tell you that she's not some old crone."

"I know she's not an old crone."

They'd reached the lake. Sigmund and the girls started changing. Markus picked up a rock and threw it. It skipped twice.

"So, what have we learned from this?" Sigmund asked as he put on his swim trunks.

"That we should never give people old lace," Ellen Christine said.

"No, that if you want something done, you have to do it yourself."

"Right. Good luck with that then," Mona said, plunging into the water along with Ellen Christine.

"I didn't mean it like that!" Sigmund shouted, following the girls.

Markus sat down on a rock and thought about what Sigmund had said. It was true, of course. He was going to have to do it himself. The next time he ran into Alexandra, he would just look deep into her eyes and say it like it was: "I love you. Take it or leave it." That's all there was to it. The more he thought about it, the simpler it got. I mean, it's not as if she was going to kill him. The world wasn't going to come crashing to a halt. Tomorrow would still come. He almost had to laugh as he sat there. Three little words. That was all. "I love you." Or maybe four: "I love you, Alexandra." He would say it. *Voila*, then it would be done. No problem. "I love you. Do you love me?" "Yes. And thanks." Or: "No, but thanks anyway." The birds were singing, the fish were jumping. It was spring. Everyone was feeling lighthearted.

"I'll say it!" he yelled so that it reverberated out over Lake Ruud.

His swimming friends looked in toward shore. He waved at them. They waved back.

"I'm going to tell her I love her!"

They kept waving, but not at him. He turned around.

Alexandra had emerged from the woods. She was wearing a tracksuit. Green this time. Well, well. Colors come and go. She had a map and around her neck was a compass on a cord.

"You again?" she asked.

He nodded. There was nowhere to hide.

"Do you have any more presents for me? An old pair of boots, maybe?"

"Heh, heh," he croaked, trying to accomplish a slight smile.

"You really think you're so funny."

"No," he said. "I, uh …"

"You, uh, what?"

"I, uh, didn't even know anything about the lace. That's totally the truth."

He realized he was still smiling.

"Thanks for a lovely afternoon," Alexandra said, running back into the woods again.

"Sure thing," Markus said, flinging himself into the water. He could use a little dip.

His friends greeted him excitedly. "Atta boy," Sigmund said.

"What did she say?" Mona asked.

"'Thanks for a lovely afternoon,'" Markus said, swimming back in toward shore.

As they dried off, he explained that he hadn't told her he loved her, just that he hadn't had anything to do with the lace.

"But now I bet she thinks *we* were the ones making fun of her," Mona lamented.

"That's the least of our problems," Sigmund said.

"Well, what's our biggest problem then?" Markus asked.

"The biggest is that she probably thinks you're in love with someone else."

"Why would she think that?"

"I'm assuming that most people who were in the woods when you yelled 'I'm going to tell her I love her!' think that," Sigmund said contemplatively. "But I'm sure we'll come up with a solution. You'd say that you were pretty embarrassed, right?"

"That's not even the half of it," Markus mumbled.

"Do you think she noticed that?"

"Yeah, unless she's blind."

"Good," Sigmund said. "That's a good start."

"For what?"

"For getting her to feel sorry for you."

"That's supposed to help?"

"Yeah," Ellen Christine said. "A lot of times girls fall in love with the boys they feel sorry for."

"How do you know that?"

"I just do."

Ellen Christine blushed, and for a second Markus thought about how much he liked her. A no-strings-attached friendship across the sexes. If only love were that easy. His thoughts were interrupted by Sigmund. "I have a plan."

Markus closed his eyes and thought about how great a sailor's life must be.

"Is it something we're going to do?" Mona asked.

"No," Sigmund said. "It's something I'm going to do. Me and Wormster."

"That sounds exciting," Ellen Christine said. "Do tell."

"I will," Sigmund said. "There's an interesting short story in *The World's Best Love Stories*. It's by Celso Al Carunungan and it's from *Like a Big, Brave Man*."

Markus, who'd just signed on to the crew of a ship in the Indian Ocean, signed off again. "I don't think that's something for me," he said.

"It starts like this," Sigmund said. "'It's very strange, but in our family love has always started with a fall of one kind or another.'"

·

It was almost dark when Markus and Sigmund walked up the road toward the subdivision. They'd said good night to Mona and Ellen Christine, who thought Sigmund had come up with a brilliant plan. Markus didn't think so, but he didn't say anything until they were alone. "That's the worst plan I've ever heard! What if I get hurt?!"

Sigmund put his arm around Markus's shoulder encouragingly. "Calm down. You're not going to hurt yourself. You'll know about it in advance."

"Yeah, but, then it'll just seem fake."

"Nah, I'll do it when you're least expecting it."

"Yeah, but, then I might hurt myself after all."

"Not seriously."

"She's going to laugh at me."

"Nah. I'm the one who'll be laughing, and then she'll probably punch me in the face, but I'm willing to take that risk for your sake. She's going to play handball tomorrow afternoon. We'll wait for her in the cafeteria, and when she walks in, I'll do it."

"It's not going to work," Markus said, relieved. "I have to be at home tomorrow."

"Why?"

"Dad invited the ear doctor to dinner."

"Surely you don't have to be home for that."

"No, I do. Dad's afraid they'll run out of things to say to each other. He's so shy."

"With his ear doctor?"

"She's a woman. I think he's in love."

"Oh, he is, is he?" Sigmund said, thinking. "Interesting."

"I'm going to help him by serving the food and then going to my room if I notice that he's starting to relax."

"This is a fantastic opportunity," Sigmund said, satisfied.

"For what?"

"To test out my plan."

"Are you crazy?! You don't mean that I'm going to …"

"No, Wormster, I'm going to do it. He's going to thank me."

CHAPTER 14 Mons dried his hands on his apron. He'd decided to serve roast lamb instead of steak. It was in the oven now, teeming with garlic. The potatoes were boiling. Two bottles of red wine were open. The nuts were in a dish on the serving cart, and the champagne was in the fridge. Still, Mons looked a little worried.

"I wasn't actually planning on inviting Sigmund," he said. "I thought it would just be the three of us."

Markus had expected this kind of reaction. That's why he'd waited until now to tell his dad. It was only a half hour until Ellen would arrive, and Sigmund was probably right around the corner.

"Relax, Dad," he said. "He's just going to help serve the food. He'll be out here in the kitchen almost the whole time."

"Well," Mons said. "I guess it's all right then, but I don't understand why he's so eager to help."

"He's practicing to be a waiter," Markus said.

"I thought he wanted to be an actor."

"Yeah, that's why he has to practice being a waiter. An actor has to learn lots of different roles."

Markus realized how idiotic that sounded, but Mons was so nervous that he didn't even bat an eye. "Well, I'm glad he's not practicing to be a murderer, at any rate," he said.

Markus laughed and said, "Good one, Dad."

The doorbell rang. Mons ran out into the hallway. Markus followed slowly behind.

"Good evening. One waiter at your service!" Sigmund bowed politely. He was wearing a dark suit, a white shirt, and a blue tie.

"Come in, Sigmund," Mons said. "You look so nice."

"Same to you, Mr. Simonsen," he replied. "Does that apron go with the suit?"

"No," Mons said. "I haven't changed yet."

"You could've fooled me," Sigmund said, following Mons into the living room. "I'll just do a quick survey of how things are going in the kitchen."

Sigmund trotted off, while Mons whispered to Markus, "Make sure he stays in there."

Sigmund stuck his head in the doorway and said, "There's quite a bit to be done in here. Come give me a hand, boy!"

Mons was about to go, but Markus held him back. "He means me, Dad. I'm his assistant waiter."

"Oh, for Pete's sake," Mons said, walking over to the cabinet to pour himself a glass of whisky.

"Good," Sigmund said. "Let's get to it. When's she coming?"

The doorbell rang.

"I think she's coming now," Markus said.

Sigmund went into the living room with Markus at his heels. Mons was already on his way to the door.

"I don't think that's wise, Mr. Simonsen."

Mons turned around. "What do you mean by that?"

"Well," Sigmund said, "it certainly is a nice apron, but still I don't think ..."

"Oh no!" Mons yelped. "I still have to change! Talk to her for a minute, won't you, Markus?" And then he said "not you" to Sigmund, who was going to open the door.

"Welcome," Sigmund said.

Ellen Bye looked a little hesitant. "Is this the right house?"

"Yes," Sigmund said jovially, "if you're the ear doctor, Dr. Bye."

"Yes, I'm Ellen Bye. Who are you?"

Markus stuck his head out from behind Sigmund and said, "That's just Sigmund."

"Oh, hi, Markus," Ellen said.

"Hi," Markus said.

"Sigmund Bastiansen Vik," Sigmund said. "May I take your coat, Dr. Bye?"

"He's training to be a waiter," Markus explained.

"You don't say!" Ellen said and turned so her back was to Sigmund.

He looked as if he didn't know what he was supposed to do.

"Aren't you going to help me off with my coat, Mr. Vik?"

"Of course," Sigmund said, pulling it off her. "Please call me Sigmund, Dr. Bye."

"And you should please call me Ellen," Ellen said, following Markus into the living room.

She looked around. "What a nice place. Where's Mons?"

"He's changing."

Now Markus saw how pretty she was. He hadn't noticed that at the doctor's office. She was a doctor then; now she was Ellen. She was definitely not over forty. Her hair was blond, her eyes blue, her lips full. She wore lipstick, but not a lot. She was wearing a black sleeveless dress with a white blouse over it and black shoes with heels that were just the right height. She was wearing a piece of silver jewelry around her neck that looked like a snake.

"You're so pretty," Markus said.

She smiled at him. "Thank you."

Sigmund came in from the hallway. "I've hung up your coat."

She smiled at him, too.

Sigmund bowed. "Please have a seat."

"Where should I sit?"

Sigmund looked as if he was a little out of it, but he did the best he could. "Oh, anywhere. *Mi casa es su casa*," he said.

She sat down on the sofa.

"Do you want something to drink?" Markus asked.

"Yes, thank you."

"We have an exquisite champagne chilling," Sigmund said, vanishing into the kitchen.

Ellen laughed. "Is he your friend, Markus?"

"Yeah. He's not as weird as he seems."

"I think he's sweet," Ellen said.

Sigmund came in with the serving cart and tried to pretend he hadn't heard what she said.

"Yes, here I come with nuts and champa … I mean … champ … here I come."

"Just relax, Sigmund," Ellen said.

"He never relaxes," Markus said.

Sigmund struggled to open the champagne bottle. The cork

hit the ceiling, and the spray hit him in the nose. He tried to act nonchalant and poured some into Ellen's glass. It foamed over.

"Sorry," he mumbled.

"No problem," Ellen said.

Then Mons came in. He was wearing gray pants, a white shirt, and a burgundy jacket. His tie was gold with a black horseshoe pattern.

"Hi, Ellen," he said. "You're here already?"

She got up and gave him a hug. "The waiter brought me a glass of champagne."

Sigmund didn't look out of it anymore. "Would you like a glass, too, Mr. Simonsen?"

"Yes, please, but you should still call me Mons."

"I think the waiter is trying to be a little more formal," Ellen said. "Isn't that right, Sigmund?"

"One does one's best," Sigmund responded and poured some champagne for Mons. "Well, Markus. I suppose we ought to check on things in the kitchen." He nodded at Mons. "Nice tie, Mr. Simonsen."

"Cheers, Mons," Ellen said.

"Cheers," Mons said.

Sigmund put the nuts on the table next to the champagne and said, "Just help yourselves."

Mons flashed a dejected look at Markus, who understood what Mons meant and tugged on Sigmund's arm. "We're going now."

"Ah yes. Will there be anything else before we retire?"

"Good-bye for now, Sigmund," Ellen said, sitting down on the sofa.

When they got to the kitchen, they heard her laughing.

"Dangerous lady," Sigmund said.

"She isn't dangerous at all. She's really nice."

"Are you sure this will work?"

"Yeah. If it doesn't work with your dad, it won't work with anyone."

"I just hope he doesn't hurt himself," Markus said, taking the lamb out of the oven.

When Markus and Sigmund entered the living room, Ellen and Mons were sitting on the sofa drinking champagne. Especially Mons. He seemed flustered and jittery and had red splotches on his cheeks.

"And the worst part of the whole thing," he said, "was that ol' Martin, that tricky devil, thought he'd been the one to trick me, but really he was the one who got tricked."

"Really, he did?" Ellen asked.

"Yes," Mons said, laughing a loud, throaty laugh that Markus recognized. "I tricked the trickster!" He took a gulp of his champagne.

"That was a funny story," Ellen said, smiling a polite but slightly curious smile.

"Dinner is served," Sigmund said.

They got up and walked over to the table. Sigmund pulled Ellen's chair out for her, and Mons whispered to Markus, "This is awful. I'm constantly making a fool of myself. I'm not used to champagne."

"You're doing just fine, Dad," Markus whispered back. "But don't drink too much red wine."

Mons shook his head and sat down.

The meal actually went quite well. Little by little Mons started to relax. He got his normal voice back, took small sips of the red wine, and chatted almost normally with Ellen about everyday things like the ringing in his ears, allergies, and the political situation in Europe. Love wasn't exactly in the air, but everyone was in a good mood. Sigmund was a discreet waiter, and Markus his helpful assistant waiter. He'd almost forgotten the whole plan and was glad that both his dad and Ellen seemed to be having a good time. When they brought the dessert in, Mons was in the bathroom.

"Your dad's very nice, Markus," Ellen said. "You, too. It's so nice to make new friends."

Sigmund cleared his throat.

"The waiter is also very pleasant," she said, winking at him, "as long as he just relaxes."

Mons came back from the bathroom. He'd combed his hair and didn't look half-bad.

"Ah, there's the ice-cream cake," he said, rubbing his hands together.

Sigmund pulled out his chair for him.

"Thank you, Sigmund," he said, sitting down.

"Ha, ha!" Sigmund exclaimed, pulling the chair out from under him in an elegant motion.

Mons tumbled onto the floor with a thump. As he fell, he grabbed his wine glass. The red wine spilled all over his pants.

At first it was quiet, then a whole bunch of things happened. Ellen leaped up and stared in bewilderment at Sigmund, who was standing over Mons with the chair in his hands. Markus ran over to them.

"What happened, Dad?"

"He pulled the chair away," Mons said, amazed.

Sigmund glanced down at him. "Did it hurt, Mr.—" He didn't get any further.

"You pulled the chair away, you underhanded little sneak! You pulled the chair away!"

Sigmund nodded. "Yes, but if you'd like to know why I ..."

Mons had gotten up onto his feet. He rubbed his butt and took a step toward Sigmund. "You pulled the chair away," he sputtered.

Sigmund set the chair back down and backed up a little. "Wouldn't you like to sit down, Mr. Simonsen?"

Then Mons exploded. He ran at Sigmund, snorting like a bull. "Get out! Out of my house, you idiot!"

Sigmund quickly darted over toward the door. "Of course, but if I could just explain ..."

"Out!"

"It was just a plan that ..."

"A plan?"

"Yes, I just thought that ..."

"Out!"

The waiter withdrew quickly and discreetly with Mons on his heels.

Ellen looked shaken. "Why in the world did he do that?"

"I don't know," Markus said. "He probably just wanted to see what would happen."

"That could be really dangerous," Ellen said.

Mons came back in.

"Did it hurt, Dad?" Markus asked nervously.

"You're asking me if it hurt?!"

"Yes."

"That's the worst thing anyone's ever done to me. I think I broke my tailbone! Has he completely lost his mind?"

"No, Dad. He did it for my sake. But now I'm sure he sees that it was a bad plan."

Markus used the little pause that arose to follow Sigmund. He caught up with him down at the intersection.

"He wouldn't even let me explain," Sigmund said indignantly. "You have to do it, Wormster, otherwise he'll think I've lost my mind."

"Yes," Markus said, "but, um, I think it's best if you don't come over to my house for a while."

"I agree. How did she take it?"

"She was really surprised."

"She didn't get a hand towel and dry his pants like Miss Rosa in 'Like a Big, Brave Man'?"

"No."

"She didn't say that I was just a scoundrel and that he shouldn't pay any attention to me either?"

"No."

"Odd. That's what Miss Rosa did. So then what did she say?"

"She said, 'That could be really dangerous.'"

Sigmund looked at him, dejected. "How was I supposed to

know that he would land so hard?" He lit up. "But all's not lost, Wormster. At least now we have confirmation that it was a bad plan."

"I have confirmation," Markus said. "*You* thought it was a good plan."

"No," Sigmund said. "Honestly, I had my doubts."

By the time Markus got home, Ellen had left. Mons was lying on the sofa with a blanket over him. Markus could tell from the look his dad gave him that he might as well tell him the truth right away. To say that Mons was an interested audience would be an understatement. He listened intently from start to finish without interrupting a single time. When everything had been said, he did something Markus would never forget. He didn't laugh. He didn't scold. He just got up from the couch, walked over to his son, and in a serious tone said, "All right."

Then he nodded and began clearing the table without asking a single question. He'd understood everything. Markus helped him clear the table. Afterward they washed the dishes. Markus didn't ask any questions either. It wasn't necessary. Mons knew how Markus felt, and Markus knew how Mons felt. It was a little sad, but there wasn't anything to be done. Mons was never going to get together with Ellen Bye.

CHAPTER 15 Mona and Ellen Christine just barely managed to convince Alexandra that no one had been making fun of her. They had misunderstood Markus. He hadn't asked them to give her lace, but rather ask her if she ever had to wear a knee brace because of orienteering. Sigmund had wondered if, while they were at it, they shouldn't mention that Markus loved her more than anything else in the world, but he decided that it was too soon. The attempt with Buster had only aroused her love for the dog. Walking back and forth in front of her house hadn't worked. The plan to pull the chair out from under Markus to elicit her compassion had been rejected. If they told her now that she was the great love of his life, it was dubious that it would have the desired effect. She wasn't ready yet. The best thing they could do now was to tell her that Markus loved Mother Nature. When Markus asked what the point to that would be, Sigmund said it was a brilliant explanation for why he'd bellowed "I'm going to tell her I love her!" by the shore of Lake Ruud.

"When she hears that you were yelling about telling Mother Nature you love her, she'll think that's just great. I mean, she's a really outdoorsy girl herself."

That's what they did. Alexandra accepted it, too, even though she thought it was a little weird that Mona and Ellen Christine told *her* that whole story.

And so a few minor problems had been solved, but the biggest one remained. Sigmund thought that Markus had made such a mess of things that it wasn't enough anymore to get her to understand that he was in love with her. They had to find a way to make Alexandra realize he was *and* to make her love him back. Maybe they'd find the answer in *Romeo and Juliet*. Mona hadn't read it yet, but it was playing at the Ruud Cineplex starring Leonardo DiCaprio and Claire Danes. The Four-Leaf Clovers went.

The story of Romeo and Juliet was beautiful and grim. They each came from different families. Romeo was a Montague and Juliet a Capulet. All the Montagues hated all the Capulets, and all the Capulets hated all the Montagues. The only ones who didn't hate each other were Romeo and Juliet. They loved each other. Yes, Markus wondered actually if Romeo didn't love Juliet as much as he loved Alexandra. Romeo and Juliet got married in secret, but then Juliet's cousin killed Romeo's best friend and then Romeo killed Juliet's cousin, but then he got kicked out of town by a prince. When Juliet found out that Romeo had killed her cousin, she was really sad, because she was extremely fond of her cousin. But when her parents insisted that she marry a guy named Paris, she was even sadder, because of course she was already married to Romeo and she liked him even more than she liked her cousin and way more than Paris. So with some help from a monk named Friar Laurence, she took a potion that made her look totally dead, even though she wasn't. Then, as was the custom, she would be laid in an open coffin in a tomb. The friar would send a note to Romeo that she was there but that she wasn't dead. After Romeo came and she woke up, they would run away to Padua, where he'd been exiled. But the plan went all wrong. Romeo found out that she was dead, but he didn't get the note, so he got himself some poison, went to the tomb, kissed her, and took the poison. When Juliet woke up and saw that Romeo was dead, she killed herself with a dagger. It was awfully gloomy. But from that day on, the two families were friends, so there's always a silver lining, as they say.

Baz Luhrmann's version of Shakespeare's tragedy was super-modern and was set in the present even though the play was written hundreds of years ago. Sigmund had read in a newspaper that the old play had been made into a movie that even today's teenagers would be able to sit through. And that's what they did.

Markus hadn't cried so much since he'd seen *Legends of the Fall*. The girls squealed and thought Leonardo DiCaprio was even cuter than Brad Pitt.

Alexandra was there, too. She sat a little in front of them, and Markus could tell from her shoulders that she cried, but she didn't squeal. Oh no, she understood what it was all about.

After the movie was over, they walked down the street toward McDonalds, while Sigmund analyzed Baz Luhrmann's version. He was merciless. "The modern effects obscure the profundity of the tragedy. An unadulterated, classic version would definitely be preferable."

The girls weren't listening. They were watching Markus, who was walking a few paces ahead of them.

"You see, Mona?" Ellen Christine asked.

"Yes," Mona said. "He walks exactly like Leonardo DiCaprio."

Sigmund looked at Markus. "I have a plan," he said.

•

"Uh, you want …" Markus got a piece of hamburger stuck in his throat. Sigmund thumped him on the back. "… you want to start a drama club and put on *Romeo and Juliet*?"

"Yes."

"And, uh, you want me to play … Romeo?"

"Yes, yes."

"And you want Alexandra to play Juliet?"

"Yes, yes, yes."

"No, no, no."

"Yes, Wormster! It's a great idea," Mona said, "isn't it, Ellen Christine?"

"Yeah, you'll get really into the part and then I'm sure she'll fall in love with you."

"I am, too," Mona said, "and when you kiss her, she'll get that you're in love with her, too."

"Kiss?" Markus croaked.

Sigmund nodded, smiling. "Yeah," he said. "The tragedy of Romeo and Juliet could have a happy ending for Wormster and Alexandra."

"But, uh … how do you know that Alexandra will want to play Juliet?"

"Obviously she'll want to," Mona said. "She's totally interested in theater."

"It's not obvious that she's so interested she'll want to play opposite me," Markus said.

"Trust us," Mona said.

"Yeah," Ellen Christine said. "You can trust us."

"Yeah, we might as well get started," Sigmund said.

"Wait a minute," Markus said.

They looked at him—Mona enthusiastically, Ellen Christine seriously, and Sigmund with a searching look. He'd already started trying to see the Romeo in Markus, who in turn was searching desperately for a way to put as much distance between himself and Romeo as possible. He found it.

"No," he said. "It won't work."

They just kept looking at him.

"It won't work, because when you put on a play you've got to rehearse, right?"

Sigmund nodded. "Yeah, only practice makes perfect."

"And I'm not going to actually be Romeo when I'm rehearsing, am I?"

Sigmund shook his head. "No, you'll be exploring the role during the rehearsals. You rehearse, you mess up, and you try again."

"That's exactly what won't work," said Markus, who was starting to feel a little more upbeat. "It would've been great if I could've just gone right in and been Romeo, but when I rehearse kissing Alexandra, I'm going to make a complete fool of myself, and then I'll be so embarrassed that I won't be able to rehearse anymore."

"Maybe you could practice on me," Ellen Christine said.

Markus had always thought she was very intelligent. Now he was starting to have doubts. "That's just silly."

"Why?" Ellen Christine looked a little hurt.

"Alexandra's certainly not going to get that I'm in love with her if you're playing Juliet."

"I'm not going to play Juliet," Ellen Christine said. Now she looked almost sad. "I'm just going to help you practice. Once you've become Romeo, you'll play opposite her."

"That's a really good idea," Sigmund said.

"That's a really bad idea," Markus said. "Because then someone else has to rehearse the part of Romeo while she's rehearsing Juliet."

Sigmund nodded. "That's right. Someone else has to do that."

"And then the other person has to get sick so that I can take over."

Sigmund nodded again. "That's what he'll have to do, all right."

"And what are the chances that he'll get sick?"

"They're pretty good," Sigmund said, "if I'm the one playing Romeo."

"Awesome," Ellen Christine said.

Mona was more skeptical. "Does that mean that you're going to kiss her when you guys rehearse?"

"No. Allow me to demonstrate," Sigmund said and put his arm around her.

"Yeah, that's best for you," Mona said, pulling away a little.

Markus knew he'd lost the war, but he kept fighting until the very end. "But what am I going to do while you guys rehearse, then? I can't just step right in without knowing what's going on."

"You'll play a minor role," Sigmund said.

"Which role?"

"A character that spends a lot of time with Juliet. Then you can study her up close, while she's rehearsing. You'll play the Nurse."

Markus started sweating. "But that's a woman!"

"Yes," Sigmund said. "That's what's ingenious about it. In Shakespeare's day men often played women. We can just say we're carrying on the tradition."

"Smart," Ellen Christine said. "Then no one will think it's weird."

"Uh-huh," Markus said. "*I'll* think it's weird."

After first period the Four-Leaf Clovers told Mr. Waage that they were thinking about starting a drama club. They wondered if it would be possible to use the gym a couple of times a week. Mr. Waage was delighted, and when Sigmund said that they were thinking of putting on *Romeo and Juliet*, there was no end to his jubilation. The principal would probably require the presence of an adult at the rehearsals, and Mr. Waage assured them that he wouldn't be at all opposed to helping out. He was already looking forward to seeing how young, creative people would interpret Shakespeare's tragedy. "Maybe there will even be a small part in it for me," he said with a shy laugh.

"You can play Friar Laurence," Sigmund said.

"Friar Laurence," Mr. Waage said and, gazing sternly at Ellen Christine, said:

> *"Hold, then; go home, be merry, give consent*
> *To marry Paris: Wednesday is to-morrow:*
> *To-morrow night look that thou lie alone;*
> *Let not thy nurse lie with thee in thy chamber."*

"No, I don't think she'll be allowing that, at any rate," Markus mumbled.

"I'm not going to be playing Juliet," Ellen Christine said.

Mr. Waage didn't hear either of them. "Umm, would you like to hear how those lines sound in Norwegian? André Bjerke's translation is magnificent," he said, staring dreamily out the window.

"Jeez, you know the Norwegian version by heart?!" Mona said, impressed.

"Yes, *Romeo and Juliet* is my favorite play. I know it in both Norwegian and English. Would you like to hear some more of the English?"

"That won't be necessary," Sigmund said. "We're going to do the play in Norwegian."

They hung up a flyer that said that anyone who was interested in being in the school's new drama club, the Shakesprentices, should come to the rehearsal for *Romeo and Juliet* in the gym, Tuesday evening at seven. Ellen Christine talked to Alexandra, who thought she'd like to go.

Apart from the Four-Leaf Clovers and Mr. Waage, about fifteen people showed up—fourteen girls and one boy named Trym Thomas, but he was only five years old. He was Turid's little brother and she'd brought him along because her mom and dad were at a party. When Sigmund explained that Alexandra was going to play Juliet, twelve of the girls left. So now there were seven of them, if they didn't count Turid's brother. The cast consisted of Mr. Waage, Ellen Christine, Mona, Alexandra, Turid, Markus, and Sigmund.

"Great," Sigmund said. "Then we'll adapt the play for seven people."

"Eight," said Trym Thomas. "I *can* count, you know."

"No, you're too little," Turid said, but Sigmund patted Trym Thomas on the head.

"No you're not. You can be Juliet's brother. That will just make it more of a tragedy."

"You have it all planned out, I see," Mr. Waage said, rubbing his hands.

CHAPTER 16 Sigmund insisted on adapting *Romeo and Juliet* by himself. Mona and Ellen Christine thought it might be a little much for him to direct, play Romeo, and adapt the play, but he explained that that was how he usually did things. By Sunday evening he was done. Mona's parents had people over, so the Four-Leaf Clovers met at Markus's house. Mons didn't have anyone over. As they were sitting down, he came into the living room and pulled the chair from under Sigmund.

"Now we're even," he said and went back to the kitchen.

Sigmund rubbed his butt, sat down cautiously, gave each actor a manuscript, and started reading.

The play had been shortened quite a bit, a number of the roles had been taken out, but it was even easier to follow the plot than in the original version. Markus and the girls were impressed. Sigmund really had managed to make a version for seven actors and a little boy.

"Well," he said when he finished reading and the applause had died down, "Shakespeare is an excellent writer, but he talks a little too much."

Then he passed out the cast list. It looked like this:

ROMEO AND JULIET
BY
WILLIAM SHAKESPEARE

(based on the Norwegian translation by André Bjerke)
ADAPTED
BY
SIGMUND BASTIANSEN VIK

ESCALUS, Prince of Verona	Turid Ytterdal
PARIS, a Young Nobleman	Turid Ytterdal
MONTAGUE, Head of the Montagues	Ellen Christine Holm
HIS WIFE	Mona Hansen
CAPULET, Head of the Capulets	Mona Hansen
HIS WIFE	Ellen Christine Holm
ROMEO, Son to Montague	Sigmund Bastiansen Vik
MERCUTIO, Kinsman to the Prince and Friend to Romeo	Mona Hansen
BENVOLIO, Nephew to Montague and Friend to Romeo	Turid Ytterdal
TYBALT, Nephew to Lady Capulet	Ellen Christine Holm
FRIAR LAURENCE, a Franciscan	Bjartmar Waage
JULIET, Daughter to Capulet	Alexandra Monsen
THOMAS, Juliet's Brother	Trym Thomas Ytterdal
NURSE TO JULIET	Markus Simonsen
DIRECTOR	Sigmund Bastiansen Vik
ASSISTANT DIRECTOR	Markus Simonsen
SCENOGRAPHY	Sigmund Bastiansen Vik
COSTUMER	Mona Hansen, Ellen Christine Holm, and Sigmund Bastiansen Vik
PROMPTER	Bjartmar Waage

"Any questions?" Sigmund asked.

"Yes," Mona said. "So, you're going to play Romeo, be the director, be in charge of the scenography ..."

"What's 'scenography'?" Markus asked.

"The sets," Sigmund said, "but I'm not going to make them. I'm just going to decide what they'll look like."

"Who's going to make them, then?" Ellen Christine asked.

"I thought I'd ask Mr. Waage."

"I'm not so sure Mr. Waage will want to make the sets," Markus said skeptically.

"No, but he could find someone to do it. Yes, Mona?"

"And then you're going to help Ellen Christine and me find the costumes?"

"No," Sigmund said. "I'm just going to decide what they'll look like."

"Oh, you will, will you?" Mona said a little sharply.

"Nah, I'm just going to help by providing advice."

"And what if we don't like your advice?"

"Then I decide," Sigmund said.

She looked at him.

"Then you guys will decide," he said meekly.

"Well, that's something at least," Mona said.

"So do you think Mr. Waage will be the prompter?" Ellen Christine asked.

"What's a 'prompter'?" Markus asked.

"The prompter whispers the lines to the actors if they forget them," Sigmund explained.

"Oh, yeah," Markus said. "I'm sure he'll want to do that. I

mean, he knows the whole play by heart and everything."

"As long as he gives us the Norwegian lines. I hope he doesn't prompt us in English," Mona said.

Sigmund stood up. "Right, then we're agreed. I'll call a read-through for Tuesday, and we'll get started."

"Shouldn't we start with the other rehearsals now?" Ellen Christine asked. "With Wormster as Romeo and me as Juliet?"

"There's no rush," Markus said, but the others thought it was a good idea, and Sigmund suggested that they should start with the masked ball at the Capulets' house, where Romeo and Juliet meet each other for the first time. They sat around the dining table, and Markus started reading:

"If I profane with my unworthiest hand

This holy shrine, the gentle fine is this ... What does 'profane' mean?"

"To make something not sacred anymore," Sigmund said. "Keep going."

"My lips, two blushing pilgrims, ready stand

To smooth that rough touch with a tender kiss. ... Should I kiss her right now?"

"Sure," Ellen Christine said.

"No," Sigmund said. "Just keep reading."

"All right," Ellen Christine said and kept going:

"Good pilgrim, you do wrong your hand too much,

Which mannerly devotion shows in this;

For saints have hands that pilgrims' hands do touch,

And palm to palm is holy palmers' kiss. ... Now you can kiss me, Markus."

"No," Sigmund said. "Keep reading."

"*Have not saints lips, and holy palmers too?*" Markus read without much feeling.

"*Ay, pilgrim, lips that they must use in prayer,*" Ellen Christine said seductively.

"*O, then, dear saint, let lips do what hands do,*" Markus continued,

"*They pray, grant thou, lest faith turn to despair.*"

"*Saints do not move, though grant for prayers' sake,*" Ellen Christine continued.

"*Then move not, while my prayer's effect I take.*

Thus from my lips, by yours, my sin is purged. ... Um, how is my sin purged?" he asked uncertainly.

"By the kiss, of course," Ellen Christine said,

"*Then have my lips the sin that they have took.*"

Markus continued, "*Sin from thy lips? O trespass sweetly urged!*"

He looked up from the book. "It says here that I should kiss her."

"Exactly," Ellen Christine said.

"So should I kiss her now?"

"That's not necessary," Sigmund said. "This is just a read-through."

"Shouldn't we just dive right into it?" Ellen Christine asked.

"Yeah," Mona said. "That makes the most sense."

"OK," Sigmund said. "Kiss her."

"I don't want to."

"Don't be a chicken," Mona said. "It's just Ellen Christine."

"Yeah," Ellen Christine said, "it's just me."

"Come on," Sigmund said. "The first time has to be sometime."

Markus thought he was right about that. He'd never kissed a girl in his whole life and hadn't imagined that the first time would be right now. On the other hand, it was just a rehearsal, not a real kiss. He glanced over at Ellen Christine, who was looking at him with a dreamy look.

"All right, then," he mumbled, and kissed her.

He'd meant to do it on her cheek, but she turned her face toward him so he kissed her mouth. He pulled back quickly, glanced down at the manuscript and whispered, "*Give me my sin again.*"

"One more time," Sigmund said.

"No!"

"Yeah. That wasn't much of a kiss."

"I did the best I could," Ellen Christine said, "but he pulled away."

"Kiss her!" Sigmund commanded.

"Why?"

"Because I said so. I'm the director."

"But I'm the one doing the kissing."

"I'll help," Ellen Christine said.

Before Markus realized what was happening, she grabbed hold of his head and pulled it in toward her.

"Grgh," he said as she pressed her lips against his.

There are lots of kinds of kisses in this world we live in: friendly kisses, loud kisses, French kisses, polite kisses, lazy kisses, cautious kisses, long kisses, short kisses, dry kisses, wet kisses, indifferent kisses, heartfelt kisses.

Markus tried to make it short. Ellen Christine tried to make it long. It ended up somewhere in the middle.

"Good, Ellen Christine," Sigmund said, "but you have to put more feeling into it, Wormster."

Markus dried his mouth and shook his head—it felt as if a bumblebee was flying around in there.

"One more time," Sigmund said.

Romeo was saved by his dad.

"What are you guys doing?" Mons asked. He'd brought some sandwiches in from the kitchen just before the second kiss.

"We're rehearsing," Sigmund said.

"Rehearsing what?"

"Kissing, Mr. Simonsen," Ellen Christine said.

"I see," Mons said.

He knew young people had their own problems, but he was a little surprised that they thought kissing required practice.

"Is it working?" he asked cautiously.

"Ellen Christine is really good at it," Mona said. "But Markus needs some more practice."

"Yeah," Sigmund said. "Practice makes perfect."

Mons set the plate of sandwiches on the table. "Yes, I suppose it does."

"We're rehearsing *Romeo and Juliet*," Markus said. "We started a drama club."

"And now we're going to take a sandwich break," Sigmund said.

Mons tried to hide his relief. "How fun," he said. "So you're playing Romeo, Markus?"

"No," Markus said. "Sigmund is. I'm just rehearsing."

"Markus has to learn the role, too," Sigmund explained. "If I get sick, he'll take over."

"Smart," Mons said. "You just never know."

Sigmund smiled at him. "True, Mr. Simonsen. You don't."

CHAPTER 17 On Monday evening Markus walked to school on his own. Sigmund had been at Mona's place all afternoon helping her with her math homework. The assignments in junior high were much harder than in elementary school, and it didn't help matters that they had to rehearse *Romeo and Juliet* at the same time. The rehearsal was supposed to start in fifteen minutes. The door was locked, and Markus started pacing back and forth across the schoolyard. He'd started rehearsing his lines already. He had a lot of lines. He had to practice both Romeo and the Nurse. He didn't quite know how he was going to keep them separate, but Sigmund had assured him that it wouldn't be a problem once they started acting. The schoolyard was empty, and Markus started wondering if the others had decided not to come after all. Wait, there was a girl over there. He quickly ducked into the bike shed, but she'd seen him and followed. There were still ten minutes left until seven o'clock, and Markus figured they were going to feel like forever.

"Hi, Markus," Alexandra said.

"Hi," Markus said. "I didn't even see you there."

It was quiet for a minute. He felt that if anyone was going to break the ice, it ought to be him.

"Dude, you're wearing your running outfit," he said.

"Yes, I am, dude," she said.

"Well, well, dude."

"Yup. I mean, we're doing our first read-through, right, dude?"

Was she making fun of him or was she shy, too?

"Yup, that we are, dude." He knew it was possible to talk without saying "dude," but he wasn't sure how to do it. "Nice weather, dude," he said.

"No. It's raining."

"Yeah, I suppose it is," he said and swallowed the word "dude."

"I guess there were a lot of artists in Paris, huh?"

She gave him a bit of a weird look, as if she thought he was making fun of her.

Markus changed the topic. "How was the wildlife?"

"Um, Paris is a city."

He nodded. "Plenty of nice weather there, I'd imagine."

"Weather?"

"Yeah, weather. In Paris. I thought maybe there was a lot of incredibly good weather there. The weather's not so great here in Ruud, I mean, and the good weather has to be somewhere."

She gave him an even weirder look. Then she started laughing. He'd managed to break the ice but unfortunately seemed to have fallen into the hole.

"Are you always like this, Markus?"

Now it was important to choose his words carefully. If he said yes, she would think he was crazy, if he said no, she would think he was making fun of her. "You can call me Wormster," he said.

She stopped laughing. "Isn't that a nickname for a little kid?"

"Yeah, but that's what everyone calls me."

"I think I'll call you Markus. If that's all right with you."

He nodded. It got quiet again. Alexandra glanced over toward the road. Markus did the same. There wasn't anyone there. She looked at her watch. He did, too. It was four minutes to seven.

She opened her backpack and fished around until she found a bottle of cola. "It's so hard to find anything in my backpack what with the knee brace in there, you know," she joked.

He didn't respond. He'd never seen anyone who drank cola as beautifully as she did. She looked at her watch again. Three minutes to seven. She put the cola in her bag and looked at the road again. Markus did the same.

"Here they come, dude," she said.

The gym was also used for end-of-the-year parties at the school. There was a stage there and a real theatrical lighting system. They'd put the table and chairs in the middle of the room and were ready for the read-through. Sigmund handed out the suggested cast list, which wasn't a suggestion but an order. Turid didn't have anything against playing the Prince, Paris, and Benvolio. Mr. Waage, who'd thought they were just kidding when they said he was going to play Friar Laurence, was as happy as could be. He said it would be no problem to get some help constructing the sets, but he was skeptical about being the prompter.

"I'm going to have enough to concentrate on with my part," he said. "Friar Laurence is a demanding role."

Trym Thomas thought it would be great to play Juliet's brother, but he didn't want to be called Thomas. "I want to be Tommy."

"We can't call Juliet's brother Tommy," Turid said.

"Then I'm going home," Trym Thomas said, "and you have to come with me."

"We can call you Tommy," Sigmund said.

"And I want to have a tiger with me," Trym Thomas insisted.

Sigmund passed out the scripts. "That you can't have, but you'll get the prologue. I was planning to give that to Juliet's brother," he explained to the others. "That'll get the play off to a good start."

"Where's a 'prologue'?" Trym Thomas asked, interested.

"It's in the script," Sigmund said. "You can just start reading."

"I can't read."

After a brief discussion it was decided that Mr. Waage would read the prologue now and then Turid would try to teach it to Trym Thomas later.

"Go ahead, Mr. Waage," Sigmund said.

Everyone except Trym Thomas opened the scripts. Mr. Waage stood up.

"You don't have to stand," Sigmund said. "This is just a read-through."

Mr. Waage sat down, inhaled and yelled, "'Two households, both alike in dignity ...'"

Trym Thomas interrupted him. "Is he a teacher?"

"Yes," Turid said.

"Then I don't want to have to go to school," Trym Thomas said and started crying.

Once Turid had comforted Trym Thomas and Sigmund had explained to Mr. Waage that he didn't have to use his full stage voice yet, they tried again. This time it went better.

"'Two households, both alike in dignity ...'" Mr. Waage repeated quietly, looking uncertainly over at Sigmund.

Now *Sigmund* was the teacher and Mr. Waage the humble student.

"Good," Sigmund said, nodding graciously.

"In fair Verona, where we lay our scene,
From ancient grudge break to new mutiny,
Where civil blood makes civil hands unclean. ..."

It turned out to be a successful read-through without any more interruptions. Alexandra and Sigmund read the lead roles without getting carried way. Markus read the Nurse without asking all the questions he thought of as they read. Mona and Ellen Christine pretended they understood everything, and Turid read her lines as best she could while trying to keep an eye on Trym Thomas. Even Mr. Waage kept his emotions under control.

Sigmund hadn't prepared anything for them to discuss. Today they were just going to familiarize themselves with the text. By nine thirty Ellen Christine, Mona, and Sigmund were pushing their bikes down the road so Markus, who hadn't brought his bike, could keep up.

"Did you guys notice how relaxed Alexandra was reading Juliet?" Sigmund asked.

"Yeah," Ellen Christine said. "But she's acted before."

"Did you notice how relaxed I was reading Mercutio?" Mona asked pointedly. "And I *haven't* acted before?"

"I think I'm going to be better as Lady Capulet than as Montague," Ellen Christine said.

"And I'm going to be really bad as the Nurse," Markus said.

"That doesn't matter," Mona said. "You're going to play Romeo."

"There, you see?" Markus said to Sigmund. "Mona thought I was bad, too."

"I did not," Mona said. "I thought you were funny."

"We all thought you were," Ellen Christine said.

"Yeah, especially Alexandra," Markus said gloomily. "When I said, 'I am a-weary, give me leave awhile: Fie, how my bones ache! what a jaunt have I had!' she started laughing."

"She'll stop laughing when she sees you as Romeo," Sigmund said. "Just pay attention to how I'm doing it."

"We'll all be paying attention," Mona said, getting on her bike. "Are you coming?"

"We're not done with the math problems yet," Sigmund explained, riding off after her.

Markus kept walking along with Ellen Christine. It had stopped raining, but there was no need for them to make small talk about the weather.

"I think you'll be great as Montague," he said.

"Do you mean it?"

"Yeah, you walk like him already."

They both laughed.

"Do you know what, Wormster? It's too bad the two of us aren't in love with each other."

"Yeah, that would've been nice."

"Maybe that's why we're not."

"Yeah," he said. "After all, being in love isn't that great."

"But we'll always be friends, right?"

"Of course. For as long as we live."

She smiled at him and got on her bike. "Bye, friend."

"Bye to you, too, friend," Markus said.

They laughed again.

Ellen Christine rode off. When she turned onto the side street where she lived, she turned and waved. He waved back. A raindrop hit his cheek.

"'Fie, how my bones ache! what a jaunt have I had!'" he said contentedly and started running.

He caught up with Mons just past the intersection.

"Hi, Markus. How'd the rehearsal go?"

He stopped running and walked along next to his dad. "It went well. Everyone was good apart from me. Did you go out, too?"

"Yeah. I went to the movies. With Ellen."

"Oh. Are you two …?"

"Nah. She probably still loves her husband."

"I thought that didn't work out."

"She probably still loves him anyway. Women are strange, aren't they, Markus?"

"They sure are, Dad. Women are extremely strange."

"But Ellen and I are getting to be good friends anyway and maybe that's just as well."

There wasn't anyone around, so Markus took his dad's hand and squeezed it. "No, Dad," he said. "It's even better."

The rain was really coming down. Markus let go of Mons's hand and started running. "Last one home makes the hot chocolate!" he yelled.

CHAPTER 18 The next few weeks were hard and went by quickly. Markus worked like a champion but didn't feel like he accomplished anything. Sigmund was starting to get a little impatient.

"When you tell Ellen Christine that you 'o'er-perched the walls with love's light wings,' you have to say it like you're in love, not like she's an old friend. Put more feeling into it! One more time!"

"All right," Markus said, positioning himself in front of Ellen Christine.

"With love's light wings did I o'er-perch these walls," he explained,
"For stony limits cannot hold love out,
And what love can do that dares love attempt;
Therefore thy kinsmen are no let to me."

To emphasize the sentiment, he gave Ellen Christine a good hug.

"No!" Sigmund yelled. "You're playing Romeo as if he were the Nurse!"

"That's how I feel it," Markus said.

On the other hand, he'd started to play the Nurse more and more as if she were Romeo, while both Markus and Mona studied the interplay between Sigmund and Alexandra. There was a lot to learn there about powerful emotions and kisses that were so pronounced you might almost think they were genuine.

When the Nurse was supposed to explain to Juliet that Romeo had killed Tybalt, Markus gazed at Alexandra with unconcealed love and whispered hoarsely:

"There's no trust,
No faith, no honesty in men; all perjured,
All forsworn, all naught, all dissemblers.
Ah, where's my man? give me some aqua vitae:
These griefs, these woes, these sorrows make me old.
Shame come to Romeo!"

"Is the point here for the Nurse to be jealous of Romeo, Sigmund?" Alexandra asked.

"No," Sigmund said. "She's not jealous."

He pulled Markus aside. "You look like you want to devour her!"

"That's how I feel," Markus said.

The only thing Markus was starting to get the hang of was the kissing. Ellen Christine always showed up faithfully. Not just to rehearsal, but also outside of rehearsals. One time she got so excited that she kissed him during break, but then Markus said they had to knock it off, otherwise people might start thinking they were a couple.

The unofficial rehearsals took place at Markus's house. Mons helped them with their lines. He'd been in drama himself once, and he'd had the job of prompter back then.

"Great!" Sigmund said. "Then maybe you could do it for our performance, too?"

Mons said he'd be happy to. He mostly sat around alone at home in the evenings anyway and thought it was fun to participate in his son's leisure activities.

Their opening performance was June 20, just before the end-of-the-year party. The problems were starting to pile up. Mr. Waage was getting anxious about how things would go with the students' final exams. The four boys he had persuaded to make the sets were working more like a chain gang than eager artisans. Trym Thomas refused to play Tommy unless he had a tiger. Mona was becoming increasingly jealous of Alexandra. Turid was having trouble learning her lines. Ellen Christine was too tired to get her homework done. The Nurse was falling deeper and deeper in love with Juliet. Mons had a lot of trouble prompting once the actors started rehearsing without the script. Sigmund's face was looking gray, and he had black circles under his eyes. He ranted and raved right and left and seemed like he was about to lose it. The only one who seemed to be having a good time was Alexandra. She was the first one to learn all her lines by heart, and she got better and better every day. Markus thought Claire Danes was amazing as Juliet, but she was nothing compared to Alexandra.

The opening was approaching. They were going to have a dress rehearsal. Mona and Ellen Christine had outdone themselves, trawling flea markets, borrowing fancy costumes from friends and relatives, getting their mothers to sew, and hunting for clothes in the attic. Sigmund had long ago given up on advising them. He was so tired that he would have approved even if they'd come to him with completely slipshod, juvenile costumes for some children's theater production of *Hakkebakkeskogen*. When they presented what they'd found, he was beside himself with enthusiasm, and when Alexandra brought in a beautiful dress she wanted to wear as Juliet, his ashen face took on a new color.

"People," he said, "I think we're going to have ourselves a show here."

"I bought a stuffed tiger for Trym Thomas," Turid said. "I hope that's all right."

"Of course not," Sigmund said. "That would give the classic tragedy a modern tone."

"We thought you could wear the costume you wore as the Silent Knight," Ellen Christine said. "Without the helmet."

"Or with it," Mona added. "We got it from your mother."

"You guys have thought of everything," Sigmund said and kissed her.

"You don't need to make a scene," Mona said and went over to help Markus with his wig. It was long and blond. Ellen Christine had borrowed it from her cousin, who'd worn it when she'd played Santa Lucia in kindergarten.

"You're going to make an interesting Nurse," Sigmund said approvingly.

Markus looked down at his costume and agreed. He was wearing a bunad, an elaborately embroidered traditional folk outfit with a long skirt that Mona had outgrown, with Mon's kitchen apron on top. His only consolation was that he would never appear in public in this getup. Ultimately, he was going to play Romeo. He glanced over at Sigmund, who was putting on the Silent Knight outfit. That was a totally different kettle of fish, but one day that kettle would be his.

"OK," Sigmund said. "Let's do a run-through of the whole play."

It's amazing what costumes can do for actors, especially for amateurs. Trym Thomas set the tone. He walked slowly out onto the stage wearing velvet pants, a white shirt, Tyrolean suspenders, and a beret. He was holding his stuffed tiger in his arms, as if he wanted to protect it against the wickedness of the world.

"'Two households, both alike in dignity,'" he said in a clear child's voice. Then he hugged his tiger to his chest and continued:

> "In fair Verona, where we lay our scene,
> From ancient grudge break to new mutiny,
> Where civil blood makes civil hands unclean.
> From forth the fatal loins of these two foes
> A pair of star-cross'd lovers take their life;
> Whole misadventured piteous overthrows
> Do with their death bury their parents' strife.
> The fearful passage of their death-mark'd love,
> And the continuance of their parents' rage,
> Which, but their children's end, nought could remove,
> Is now the two hours' traffic of our stage;
> The which if you with patient ears attend,
> What here shall miss, our toil shall strive to mend."

He gazed lovingly at his tiger. Then he bent his head and kissed it. After that he left the stage. The gym had grown completely silent. Trym Thomas probably didn't understand an ounce of what he'd just said, but he'd learned all the strange words by heart and performed the prologue with true affection. For the tiger. Markus, who was standing backstage, heard someone sniff out in the audience. It was the prompter. Behind him a deep voice was chanting "mar-may-moo-mee-mor." That was Mr. Waage doing his voice warm-up exercises. In a long, black raincoat and patent leather shoes.

The rehearsal moved along in the tone set by Trym Thomas. All of them acted as they never had before. The famous balcony scene where Romeo visits Juliet in her garden was wonderful. The girls switched back and forth between their roles elegantly, even if the changes were sometimes a little slow, but they did their best. It was their first dress rehearsal. Even the Nurse managed to hide how in love she was under her wig and bunad. Still, Markus knew everything would fall apart, and when it did, it really fell apart.

It happened when the Nurse came to Juliet to tell her that everything was ready for her secret marriage to Romeo. Markus came running onto the stage with his wig flying, puffing like an ox. Alexandra grabbed hold of both his hands and looked at him tenderly with one green and one brown eye.

"Now, good sweet nurse,—O Lord, why look'st thou sad?
Though news be sad, yet tell them merrily;
If good, thou shamest the music of sweet news
By playing it to me with so sour a face."

He stared into her eyes and couldn't say a word. He knew that

that tender look wasn't for him, but for Romeo, but still, she was looking at *him*. First tenderly and then a little uncertainly. Oh, God, she was so gorgeous! Her eyes sparkled. Green and brown. The most beautiful colors in the world. From far away he heard Mons whisper, "'I am a-weary.'"

It was as if her eyes were getting bigger and bigger.

"'Give me leave awhile,'" Mons whispered a little louder.

As if they were changing colors as he looked at them.

"'Fie, how my bones ache! what a jaunt have I had!'" Mons prompted.

Now the green eye was brown and the brown one green.

"'I am a-weary, give me leave awhile: Fie, how my bones ache! what a jaunt have I had!'" Mons yelled.

Markus opened his mouth.

"But, soft!" he said. *"What light through yonder window breaks?*

It is the east, and Juliet is the sun.

Arise, fair sun, and kill the envious moon,

Who is already sick and pale with grief,

That thou her maid art far more fair than she:

Be not her maid, since she is envious;

Her vestal livery is but sick and green

And none but fools do wear it; cast it off.

It is my lady, O, it is my love!

O, that she knew she were!

She speaks yet she says nothing: what of that?

Her eye discourses; I will answer it.

I am too bold, 'tis not to me she speaks:
Two of the fairest stars in all the heaven,
Having some business, do entreat her eyes
To twinkle in their spheres till they return.
What if her eyes were there, they in her head?
The brightness of her cheek would shame those stars,
As daylight doth a lamp; her eyes in heaven
Would through the airy region stream so bright
That birds would sing and think it were not night.
See, how she leans her cheek upon her hand!
O, that I were a glove upon that hand,
That I might touch that cheek!"

Trym Thomas had impressed everyone with the prologue, but Markus made no less of an impression with Romeo's declaration of love performed in the Nurse's costume. The prompter rose from his chair. The actors came out onstage. No one said anything. Everyone stared. Markus had played Romeo with a level of feeling they had never known before, without even thinking about the audience. He and Alexandra were the only ones in the whole world. He was in heaven, and her eyes twinkled like stars. Her mouth was half-open. Her lips red. He brushed his wig hair off his face, closed his eyes, and opened his mouth.

"Thank you," Sigmund said. "We'll stop there."

Markus blinked his eyes. He felt a little dazed. Where was he? What time was it? He looked around the room in confusion. Oh, there was his dad.

"That wasn't quite right," Mons said quietly. "You were actually supposed to say, 'I am a-weary, give me leave awhile: Fie, how my bones ache! what a jaunt have I had!'"

"Oh, whoops," Markus mumbled and ran out of the gym.

If he'd stayed a little longer, he would have heard Ellen Christine and Mona clapping.

CHAPTER 19 Markus heard the phone ringing when he opened the front door. He closed it again and stood there out on the steps and waited a little. Then he opened the door again. The phone rang. He closed the door, opened it, sighed, went into the living room and answered it.

"Hello."

"Wormster?"

It was Ellen Christine.

"Yeah."

"Where'd you go?"

"I went home."

"Why?"

"What do you think?"

"You were amazing!"

"Bye."

"Wait."

"Why?"

"Everyone's talking about you."

"Yeah, I figured as much."

"You were better than Leonardo DiCaprio."

"Quit messing with me!"

"Alexandra said that she'd never seen anyone play Romeo with that kind of emotion."

"No. Especially not the Nurse."

"She was totally mesmerized. You shouldn't have left!"

Markus didn't get what was going on. This wasn't the first time he'd made a fool of himself, but on his top-ten list of foolish behavior, this obviously ranked number one. It wasn't just dumb. It was absolute, total idiocy. And then she said that it was fantastic! Ellen Christine wasn't lying. He could tell from her voice. But if she wasn't lying, then that must mean the more he thinks he makes a fool of himself, the more fantastic other people think he is, and that must mean that the less he makes a fool of himself, the more other people think he's making a fool of himself, and if that's how things were, then the whole point to life was to make as much of a fool of himself as possible.

"Wormster!" the voice on the phone said.

"Hello."

"Are you still there?"

"I think so."

"We had to stop the rehearsal."

Finally a sentence he understood. "I realize that."

"Sigmund got hurt."

"What?"

"When you ran out, he went over to the edge of the stage and he was standing there, kind of pacing around. And then he fell off and sprained his ankle." She giggled.

"Well, that's certainly no reason to laugh!"

"It is so, because now someone else has to play Romeo, don't they?"

"Who … No!"

"Yeah! The plan worked! Everyone wants you to take over the part now. Sigmund says that was a great prompt you gave him."

"That wasn't a prompt. It just turned out that way."

"Nothing just turns out *that way*."

"I didn't do it on purpose."

"Wait a minute, Wormster." And then to someone else she says, "He says that he didn't do it on purpose. Yeah, good point." To Markus she says, "Sigmund says that it isn't possible to do what you did without doing it on purpose."

"Is Sigmund there?"

"Yeah, we're over at Mona's house."

"I thought he hurt his ankle."

She giggled again. "Yeah, I'm sure you do think that. Are you coming over?"

"Now?"

"Yeah. We have to talk about who's going to play the Nurse."

"No one's going to play the Nurse," Markus said and hung up. He ran into the hallway. He had to hurry, before they put ads in all the newspapers in the country that Markus Simonsen was going to play Romeo at Ruud School on June 20.

He ran into Mons at the door.

"You sure get around, Markus," he said. "Where are you off to now?"

"Mona's house."

"Should I come and listen to your lines?"

"I'm not going to be acting," Markus said. Then he opened and closed the door three times and disappeared down the street. Mons opened the door one more time. Then he closed it and went into the living room. *His* lucky number was four.

Sigmund opened Mona's front door. He looked as if he was in perfect health. "'Now, good sweet nurse,—'" he said, satisfied. "'O Lord, why look'st thou sad? Though news be sad, yet tell them merrily.'"

"I refuse!"

"You refuse what?"

"To play Romeo."

"Are you crazy?! You're going to be magnificent!"

"I'm going to pass out is what I'm going to do."

"No. The girls are going to do that."

"They will not. We're canceling the whole thing."

"No way. We've all worked like crazy on this for your sake. Ellen Christine is getting worse grades at school. I've worn myself ragged. Mona is so jealous of Alexandra she's about to break up with me. You were the one who started this whole thing."

"No, that was you."

"You're the one who fell in love," Sigmund said.

"Well, excuse me!"

"That's not going to cut it. We've sacrificed everything for your sake. If you leave us hanging now, you can just forget about us."

"But, Sigmund …"

"Everyone's looking forward to seeing you as Romeo. We brought the costume. You can try it on now."

"I'm sure it won't even fit," Markus mumbled and followed Sigmund to where Mona and Ellen Christine were.

It fit pretty well, although the velvet jacket was a little too big, and the leggings weren't quite as tight on him as on Sigmund.

"Oh, you're so cute," Mona said.

"Really cute," Ellen Christine said. "Do you want to do a little practice kissing?"

Markus shook his head. "Couldn't I wear the helmet, too?"

All three of them laughed, and Markus realized there was no point in telling them he'd been serious.

"Now, there's the question of the Nurse," Sigmund said. "We have a problem there."

"Oh, darn," Markus said. "We have no Nurse. We're going to have to cancel the show anyway."

"I have an idea," Sigmund said.

The next afternoon they held a Nurse meeting at Markus's house. Mona and Ellen Christine brought the costume. Sigmund was wearing an ankle brace and had pulled a sock over his sneaker. He was also using a pair of crutches that made his injury seem serious. He'd presented his idea to Mons, who mostly looked as if he wanted to emigrate.

"You … you want me to …"

"Yes," Sigmund said. "I admit, it's a desperate measure, but it's the only way out."

"I don't want to! The bunad is too small." Mons said.

"I borrowed my mom's," Mona said, suddenly looking like she was nineteen.

"Please, Mons. You'll be very handsome."

"I will not," Mons said a little more gently.

"For our sakes?" Ellen Christine asked, looking like she was twenty.

"I don't think …"

"And for your son's?" Sigmund said.

Markus smiled wanly. "You don't have to, Dad," he whispered.

Mons misread what Markus wanted him to do. "All right," he sighed. "I might as well try the costume on."

"That's the spirit, Mr. Simonsen," Sigmund said.

"On the condition that you stop calling me Mr. Simonsen."

Sigmund nodded solemnly. "It would be an honor to call you Mons."

"Jeez," Mons mumbled, and disappeared into the bathroom with the bag containing the costume.

When he came back in again, the Four-Leaf Clovers studied him somberly. Sigmund had said that if they laughed, the whole plan would fail. Then Mons would refuse no matter how much they begged and pleaded. The only one who was genuinely serious was Markus. He and his dad were so alike that he knew exactly how his dad was feeling.

"You look great, Mons," Ellen Christine said, her voice sounding a little funny.

"As if you were made for the part," Mona said. "Mom's bunad fits perf … Excuse me a second. I have something in my throat." She disappeared into the bathroom. Ellen Christine ran after her.

"Interesting," Sigmund said. "An older, slightly exhausted Nurse."

Exhausted was the word. Two anxious eyes peeked out from

underneath the Santa Lucia wig. His forehead was wrinkled and his mouth drawn. The girls came back from the bathroom more serious than ever. Mona went over to Mons and adjusted his wig a little. He hadn't said anything since putting on the costume. Now he looked over at Markus a little hesitantly. "What do you think? Am I OK?"

"Yes, Dad. You're totally OK," Markus said seriously.

"Try one of your lines," Sigmund said.

Mons looked at him for a long time and then sighed. "'I am a-weary, give me leave awhile: Fie, how my bones ache! what a jaunt have I had!'"

Sigmund looked around triumphantly.

"Could anyone say it better?"

It certainly wasn't said better the next day at the dress rehearsal. Markus was unrecognizable. He'd totally lost his inspiration and was shier than ever. No one, not even Alexandra, could hear a word of what he said, and kissing was out of the question. Quite the contrary: it was clear that Romeo was trying to avoid Juliet as best he could. Each time she came closer, he pulled away, brooding and gloomy. When Alexandra said it was impossible to act with him when he kept pulling away like that, Sigmund, who was sitting with his leg up on a chair and prompting, explained that that was how Markus worked.

"When you play a bad guy, you always have to search for the good sides of the role. When you play a hero, you have to figure out how he's a coward. That makes the character complex and gives it depth. Good, Markus!"

"I hope he's finished working on the character's complexity by the opening," Alexandra said and called to Markus, who was on his way offstage, "'O Romeo, Romeo! wherefore art thou Romeo?'"

If Romeo wasn't quite up to par, the Nurse wasn't any better. Mons wandered around, looking lost. He mixed up his lines, lost his wig, and tripped on the skirt of his bunad, but the worst thing of all was that the problems Romeo and the Nurse were having seemed to be making everyone else's performances worse. The cast was turning into a flock of hens, with everyone nagging each other and no one knowing what to do with themselves. The only consolation was that their artistic decline was a hit with the audience. Mr. Waage's carpentry workers, who hadn't shown any particular interest in the show so far, were now following along eagerly. They were clapping and laughing and really getting into it every time the Nurse messed up. Finally Mons couldn't take any more. He sat down on the stage with a thump.

"I'm sorry," he said. "I can't do this."

"Maybe I can help."

No one had noticed her come in, but she'd been standing in the back of the room watching for quite a while. Markus had seen her only twice before, but he hadn't noticed then how similar to Alexandra she was. Now he saw it. She had the same dark hair, the same look in her eyes, and the same deep voice.

The carpenters stopped laughing. Sigmund forgot his bum leg and leaped up. Then he remembered it, said an exaggerated "ow!", and sat down again.

"Yeah, Mom," Alexandra said. "I think you can. You played

Juliet in theater school. I'm sure you could play the Nurse, too."

Mons was still sitting on the stage. "You …," he said. "You …"

Alexandra's mother walked up to the stage. "I'd be happy to do it if you guys want," she said, nodding at Mons. "But I don't mean to steal your part from you."

Mons leaped to his feet, stepped on the bunad skirt, and stumbled over to the edge of the stage.

"No, no," he said, "it's perfectly all right. It's so nice …"

"I'm Sara Monsen," she said, smiling at him.

"Really? My name is actually Monsen, too! Um, I mean … Mons." He took the wig off and scratched his head. Markus noticed that he'd started croaking.

Sara laughed. "I'm Alexandra's mom," she said, holding out her hand.

"And I'm Markus's dad," Mons croaked.

"I knew that, actually," she said, looking into his eyes.

"Uh," Mons whispered and was saved by Mr. Waage.

"All right everybody. I think we'll have to wrap this up. It's past ten, and 8B has an English exam tomorrow."

Sigmund got up. "OK, everybody. Thanks for all your work tonight. Go home and relax. This is going well. I think we're on our way to putting on a play here!"

CHAPTER 20 The opening performance was approaching. Sigmund was starting to gather all the threads together in his sweaty hand. Mons was doing the prompting, so that was a delight. Trym Thomas had gotten so much praise that he was starting to get a little full of himself. In particular he kept criticizing Mr. Waage, who he thought acted like a sleazeball. Friar Laurence had developed an obvious dislike for the young Tommy Capulet, but Sigmund thought that just added yet another exciting conflict to the drama. Turid's, Ellen Christine's, and Mona's parts had gotten an extra lift once Sigmund had the lighting all set up. Markus wasn't trying to escape from Alexandra anymore. On the other hand, he was as stiff as a board and received her kisses with his eyes closed and his lips pursed while he tried to think of something else. Still, Alexandra was able to make it look almost genuine. She'd long ago given up hope of getting more of the kind of acting he'd given her in the Nurse's costume, but she did her best with the situation, and it was working in a way.

Sara Monsen was a great Nurse, even though Markus thought she was maybe a little too elegant. Somewhere between the Nurse and a queen. He told Sigmund that as they walked home after a long rehearsal.

The director, who was still walking with crutches, gave him a condescending look. "Have you ever seen a nurse, Wormster?"

"Well, no, but …"

"Then you shouldn't leap to conclusions."

"No, but …"

"Maybe you should concentrate on your own part instead. Tomorrow's the dress rehearsal."

"I can't do it," Markus said unhappily.

Sigmund changed tactics. Biting criticism wasn't working anymore. Now it was a matter of building up the boy's self-confidence. "You have him in you, Wormster," he said, putting his arm around Markus's shoulder. "All you have to do now is let him out. Quit stressing out. Relax. Enjoy yourself—enjoy the role." He raised one of his crutches in a wave and limped away cheerfully.

Markus stood there for a second trying to enjoy himself as best he could. Then he went home.

Mons had beaten him home and was already changed. For some reason or other he'd started wearing his best clothes when he was working as the prompter. When Markus walked into the living room, Mons was sitting on the sofa reading. "Is that you, Markus?" he asked without looking up from his book.

"Yeah. Are you enjoying yourself, Dad?"

"No, I'm reading."

"What are you reading?"

"*The Sorrows of Young Werther.*"

"I already returned that."

Mons nodded absentmindedly. "I borrowed it again."

He looked up at Markus, who thought his dad would actually have made a good Romeo if he'd been younger and looked a little different.

"You think it's *that* good?"

Mons smiled an indescribably sad and, at the same time, longing smile. "Listen to this, Markus. 'How her image haunts me! Awake or asleep she is ever present to my soul!—Soon as I close my eyes, here in this brain, where all my nerves are concentered, her dark eyes are imprinted. Here—I don't know how to describe it!'" He picked up a handkerchief and blew his nose.

"I know what you mean," Markus said, going into his room.

He lay there, staring at the ceiling. Relax. Enjoy yourself—enjoy the role. "Awake or asleep she is ever present to my soul." Awake or asleep. Asleep. Sleep. There was something there. Asleep, asleep, sleep. That's what he'd done as the Nurse: he had played Romeo in his sleep. He'd gotten lost in a dream. He could do that again. That was maybe the only thing he could do. He had to pretend everything was a dream. As if the whole play was just a dream. His dream. His dream about Alexandra. That's what Sigmund had meant when he told him to relax. In his sleep, when he was dreaming, he was always relaxed. He closed his eyes and whispered, "'With love's light wings did I o'er-perch these walls.'"

Then he fell asleep. In his dream he found his inner Romeo.

Ten minutes were left until the dress rehearsal. Sigmund had invited the actors' families to watch. The mood backstage was hectic and nervous. Most of the parents were sitting several rows back in the room, but Sigmund asked them to move up to the front row, next to Mrs. Waage. She was a teacher, too, and had brought paper and a pencil so she could give her husband comments after the rehearsal. Markus was standing backstage with his eyes closed, concentrating on the dream.

The curtain went up, and Trym Thomas walked onto the stage. "Hi, Mom," he said. "I'm doing good, huh?"

The curtain came down and they tried again.

This time it went better. In a cheerful way Sigmund had explained to Trym Thomas that he would shoot the tiger if the boy didn't say the lines he was supposed to say.

The audience clapped every time someone walked on- or offstage, and the actors performed their parts with renewed self-confidence. Markus felt surprisingly light when he went in to meet Juliet for the first time. She was standing on the other side of the stage with Mona, who was playing Capulet. She looked into his eyes. Markus sank into the dream and said:

"*O, she doth teach the torches to burn bright!*
It seems she hangs upon the cheek of night
Like a rich jewel in an Ethiope's ear;
Beauty too rich for use, for earth too dear!
So shows a snowy dove trooping with crows,
As yonder lady o'er her fellows shows.
The measure done, I'll watch her place of stand,
And, touching hers, make blessed my rude hand.
Did my heart love till now? forswear it, sight!
For I ne'er saw true beauty till this night."

The audience applauded. He didn't hear. Ellen Christine, who was playing Tybalt, and Mona, who was playing Capulet, said their lines. He didn't hear them. He walked slowly across the stage and over to Alexandra. Her eyes gleamed. He held out his hand to her. She took it. He pulled her hand to him, held it to his lips and whispered just loud enough for the audience to hear every word:

> *"If I profane with my unworthiest hand*
> *This holy shrine, the gentle fine is this:*
> *My lips, two blushing pilgrims, ready stand*
> *To smooth that rough touch with a tender kiss."*

Then Markus Romeo Simonsen pulled Alexandra Juliet Monsen in close and kissed her. She was a dream in his arms.

He was still holding onto her when their lips slid apart. He smiled at her. She smiled at him. Then she opened her mouth. "'Good …,'" she said in a strangely hoarse voice that ended in a slight squeak. She closed her mouth. Opened it again. "'Good …'"

It sounded like a chicken in distress.

"'Good pilgrim,'" Mons whispered from the wings.

Alexandra looked at Markus in dismay. "I've lost my …," she whispered.

"'Good pilgrim,'" Mons called valiantly.

"… voice," Alexandra squeaked and ran offstage.

Trym Thomas had gone home along with his parents, Mr. Waage went out to eat with his wife, but the rest of the actors held an emergency meeting. Sara was afraid her daughter had come down with tonsillitis. She'd had a bit of a sore throat all week. They'd hoped it would go away on its own, but now there was no way she would be able to act in the opening. This was absolutely the worst thing that could happen. Alexandra was crushed, and Sigmund, who almost always had an idea, for once had absolutely no idea what they were going to do. The opening performance was sold out. There was no stopping the local paper. Sigmund had already been interviewed under the headline: "Local Junior High's Jack-of-All-Trades." And now they had to cancel the whole thing. Sigmund had created the performance of his dreams. Markus had found his Romeo. Everything had gone the way it was supposed to. Sigmund had come up with a plan and it was a success. The opening would have been an enormous success. A well-deserved feather in the cap of the Local Junior High's Jack-of-All-Trades. Now everything was ruined.

Mona sat down next to him and stroked his hair. "Don't be upset, Sigmund," she whispered. "You did your best."

Then a hoarse voice whispered, "Mom." Everyone except Sigmund looked at Alexandra. She was pointing to her mother.

"I think she means that I could play Juliet," Sara said.

Alexandra nodded.

Sigmund rose up from his grave. "Do you know the part?"

"If you guys think it will save the show, I could certainly give it a try. I did play the role once, but I don't know if I remember all the lines. Maybe Mons could help me with it."

Mons adjusted his tie a little. "I'm at your dispose."

Sara smiled at him. "My dispose?"

"Disposal," Mons said, laughing a high, croaking laugh.

"But then who will play the Nurse now?" Ellen Christine asked.

"I have an idea," Sigmund said.

Mons stopped laughing.

It was after one a.m., but Mons hadn't come home yet. He'd gone home with Sara to hear her lines. Markus had gone to bed, but he couldn't sleep. He felt so strangely empty. The dream had become real. The kiss was kissed. And in a way, that was that. Alexandra was just as pretty as before. He still loved her more than anyone else in the whole world, but that wasn't so strange since he didn't love anyone else. When she felt better, he could kiss her again. No problem. It would probably all be fine. Time was moving along. Today he was a day older than he was yesterday. He read in *Words about Love*, "Who can doubt after this whether we are in the world for anything else than to love?" The quote was from Blaise Pascal, and Markus assumed he knew what he was talking about. Still, it couldn't *just* be about love. There were other things, too, of course: food, books, good movies, and friendship. His friendship with Sigmund, for example, and with Ellen Christine. Surely he wasn't here in the world just to love Alexandra. Surely he was here to be friends with Ellen Christine, too.

He heard the front door open and went into the living room.

Mons had red splotches on his cheeks and was talking up a storm. "Ah, so, you're not asleep yet? I'm supposed to say hi. I have to tell you that Sara is quite an actor. She's going to be positively magnificent. Believe it or not, she knew almost all the lines. I didn't have to prompt her at all. I just had to look at her, so she had someone to act to. When we were done, we had a glass of wine. Did you know she's planning on starting a theater company? I signed up, I did. It would appear that I've caught the acting bug, and it'll be a good diversion from work, don't you think? She's thinking of putting on *Hamlet*. She'll play the queen, and she says she has a role for me, too. What do you say to that, Markus?"

"Good," Markus said. "What role will you play?"

"I'm going to play the king's ghost. That's an important part, of course. I think it'll be fun."

"I'm sure it will, Dad," Markus said. "But first you're going to play the Nurse."

"I think I'm going to bed," Mons said.

CHAPTER 21 The opening was going to start at eight o'clock. The audience started arriving at seven. At seven thirty, Mrs. Waage opened the doors and started handing out the new cast list Sigmund had made. It looked like this:

ROMEO AND JULIET
BY
WILLIAM SHAKESPEARE
(based on the Norwegian translation by André Bjerke)
ADAPTED BY
SIGMUND BASTIANSEN VIK

ESCALUS, Prince of Verona	Turid Ytterdal
PARIS, a Young Nobleman	Turid Ytterdal
MONTAGUE, Head of the Montagues	Ellen Christine Holm
HIS WIFE	Mona Hansen
CAPULET, Head of the Capulets	Mona Hansen
HIS WIFE	Ellen Christine Holm
ROMEO, Son to Montague	Markus Simonsen
MERCUTIO, Kinsman to the Prince and Friend to Romeo	Turid Ytterdal
BENVOLIO, Nephew to Montague and Friend to Romeo	Turid Ytterdal
TYBALT, Nephew to Lady Capulet	Ellen Christine Holm

FRIAR LAURENCE, a Franciscan	Bjartmar Waage
JULIET, Daughter to Capulet	Sara Monsen
THOMAS, Juliet's Brother	Trym Thomas Ytterdal
NURSE TO JULIET	Mons Simonsen
DIRECTOR	Sigmund Bastiansen Vik
ASSISTANT DIRECTOR	Markus Simonsen
SCENOGRAPHY	Sigmund Bastiansen Vik
COSTUMER	Mona Hansen
	and Ellen Christine Holm
COSTUME CONSULTANT	Sigmund Bastiansen Vik
PROMPTER	Sigmund Bastiansen Vik

There was room for two hundred and fifty people in the gym. Three hundred and fourteen came. Students and parents. Relatives and friends. There was standing room for some of them in the very back of the room. Those who didn't get in were clustered around the window outside. When Sigmund closed the curtains, a disappointed howl could be heard from outside. He opened them a crack, and the competition for a window spot began. There was a buzz of voices and the crinkling of candy wrappers. The curtain parted. A pale face peeked out at the room, and the teenagers in the audience chanted, "Woohoo, Mr. Waage! Woohoo, Mr. Waage!"

The head disappeared.

Sigmund hobbled up onto the stage.

"Woohoo, Sigmund! Woohoo, Sigmund!"

He bowed. "Ladies and gentlemen. Principal Dahl."

"And Your Royal Highness," a faint voice in the room called out.

Sigmund smiled charmingly. "It's a pleasure for us, the members of the Shakesprentices, to present the great classic drama of *Romeo and Juliet*. ..."

"Woohoo, Sigmund! Woohoo, Sigmund!"

He tried to quiet them with a disapproving wave. "We hope you will spend a few exciting hours here with us. Enjoy the show."

Applause! Cheers!

Sigmund came back down off the stage and sat in the front row between the principal and Alexandra.

The lights went down. Silence settled over the gym.

"Let the show begin," Sigmund said.

Nothing happened.

"Let the show begin!"

Trym Thomas came stumbling out from between the curtains.

Applause!

"I lost my tiger!" Trym Thomas screamed.

Mr. Waage came running out.

Fresh applause.

"It's right here, you little ... I have it here, boy," he said.

Trym Thomas snatched the tiger and clasped it to his chest.

"The teacher stole it," he explained to his friend Tormod, who was the same age as him and was sitting in the front row. "He's a sleazeball."

Mr. Waage smiled wanly at the audience, put his hand behind Trym Thomas's head, and steered him back through the curtains.

The audience clapped.

"Is it over already?" Tormod asked.

Then Mrs. Waage raised the curtain.

Trym Thomas was standing alone on the stage with an angelic smile. He was holding the stuffed tiger over his head so everyone could see it, and he began, "'Two households, both alike in dignity ...'"

Well, what is there to say? The opening went very well. When the Nurse fell on her face for the first time, the audience really got into the spirit of things. The Nail, who was sitting behind Sigmund, laughed so much he almost fell out of his chair, and Principal Dahl whispered, "Great idea, Sigmund. Making the Nurse into a male clown. Very funny."

Sigmund, who was sitting there chewing on his lower lip, nodded. "Yes, I tried to give this somber tale a cheerier undertone."

Then came the first meeting between Romeo and Juliet. This caused some uneasiness. As individuals, both Markus and Sara Monsen did quite well. Sara acted with an intensity and a desire that made quite an impression. No one could have any doubt that she was deathly in love with Romeo. Markus started out more reserved, almost shy. But he gradually came alive, and soon he was playing Romeo with the ardor one finds in a young person experiencing his first great love. Strangely enough, it was precisely this powerful interaction that caused the adult members of the audience in particular to murmur. This unabashed love between a woman of over forty and a boy of fourteen gave the show a bit of an unsavory twist. It wasn't made any better by the fact that the

Nurse kept glaring at them. An obviously jealous transvestite did not help give the show the decorum Shakespeare's words called for.

The teenagers in the audience stared so hard their eyes were almost popping out. Some of the grown-ups started clearly expressing their disapproval. The principal's face was white, Sigmund's was red, and the Nail looked as if he was choking on something. When the first kiss came, Tormod's mother stood up and left the room along with her son.

They kept acting their way through to the intermission. The discussion in the schoolyard was heated, but no one else left. Everyone wanted to stay and see how this madness would end.

Principal Dahl walked into the dressing room with Sigmund and Alexandra at his heels. He wanted to talk to Mr. Waage.

"This is …," he said. "This is …"

"Yes? So, what do you think?" Mr. Waage asked enthusiastically. "Not bad, huh?"

He'd been concentrating so much on his part that he hadn't noticed the signs from the audience.

"Not bad?" Principal Dahl hissed. "It's perverse!"

Everyone, except for Trym Thomas, was unhappy. Mr. Waage tried to apologize, explaining that cast list had changed so many times he'd given up trying to keep track of who was playing which part. That didn't go well. So Sara tried to charm the principal. When that didn't go well either, she explained that she had stepped in because her daughter was sick. Alexandra whispered hoarsely that she could try to do the rest of the play anyway. Sara said no. Sigmund said that if Principal Dahl insisted, they could stop the performance. Principal Dahl said that the damage had already been done. The journalist from the local paper had been jotting down notes like crazy. Quitting now would just emphasize the scandal.

"Somehow or other …," Sigmund said. "Somehow or other, you're going to have to grin and bear it."

"Or grin and wear it," Mons mumbled, fiddling with the skirt of his bunad.

"What did you say, Mr. Simonsen?"

Mons shook his head and went out the back door to smoke a cigarette.

"I demand an explanation," Principal Dahl said, "and I demand another performance!"

With that he left the dressing room, leaving the unsolvable problem to the Shakesprentices.

Mons came back in. "Did he leave?"

Markus nodded.

"He wasn't very happy," Mons said, heading back over to his corner.

Everyone was looking at Sigmund. He swallowed and swallowed. "My dear friends," he said.

No one answered.

"This is my responsibility." He looked around to see if anyone would protest. No one did. "Before you start, I'll explain to the audience why it turned out this way."

"I don't think it's such a good idea for us to keep acting," Markus said.

"You guys aren't going to act," Sigmund said softly. "You're going to prove a point."

"But then the show will be a flop, won't it?" Mona asked.

Sigmund nodded heavily. "Yes," he said. "You're going to do as bad a job as you can." For a guy whose ambition was to become a new Ingmar Bergman, this was a terrible thing to say. "Just read the lines," he continued. "Stand up straight. Don't look at each other. Don't touch each other. Don't ... kiss each other."

Markus nodded. "I get what you mean," he said.

"It's a shame," Sara said, "but I think you're right."

Mr. Waage took off his raincoat. "This will keep me from getting too carried away playing the friar," he explained.

"I can play Juliet," Ellen Christine said.

"What did you say?" Sigmund, who had sat down on a bench to write his farewell speech to the audience, leaped up again.

"I mean, I *have* been practicing it with Markus."

"You have?" Alexandra whispered.

"She's just been helping him with the lines," Mona explained.

"And teaching him to kiss," Ellen Christine said.

"Urg," Markus said.

Alexandra looked at him for a long time.

But Sigmund's face had taken on a new radiance. He started pacing back and forth across the floor and muttering. "It's possible, it's possible, it's ... Should we do it?"

Markus shook his head. "It won't work. If Ellen Christine plays Juliet, we don't have anyone who can play Montague, Lady Capulet, and Tybalt."

"Yes we do!" Sigmund said. "We have someone!"

"No," Mr. Waage said. "I have more than enough already with Friar Laurence."

"I didn't mean you. I meant me," Sigmund said triumphantly.

"But you hurt your leg," Turid said.

Sigmund threw down his crutches and took off his sock. "I'm much better now," he said. "Come on, people, we have a costume change to do." He gave the script to Sara. "Would you mind taking over the prompting?"

She smiled at him. "It would be an honor."

Sara's costume was too big for Ellen Christine, so she switched clothes with Alexandra, who was wearing the dress *she* had played Juliet in. It fit perfectly. The clothes for Montague, Lady Capulet, and Tybalt were on the small side, but Sigmund sucked in his gut and buttoned what he could. The second act was fifteen minutes late, but the audience waited.

When Sigmund came out onto the stage in Tybalt's tight-fitting pants, a couple of ninth-grade girls even whistled.

"Dear audience," he said. "We owe you a bit of an explanation."

Principal Dahl adjusted his tie, and the rest of the audience watched Sigmund, some in disgust, others in eager anticipation.

"We've made a few changes to the cast. Due to illness, Sara Monsen was kind enough to play Juliet."

Some of the oldest boys clapped but were quickly shushed.

"It was a last-ditch solution," Sigmund explained. "And it was never the intention that she would do more than the first act," he laughed heartily.

Two of the boys who had clapped started booing but were silenced again.

"For the next four acts, Juliet will be played by Ellen Christine Holm, and Montague, Lady Capulet, and Tybalt by Sigmund Bastiansen Vik. Enjoy the rest of the show!" He bowed and waited for the applause. It didn't come. Sigmund went back behind the curtain.

"I thought he broke his leg," Principal Dahl whispered to Sara.

"Yes," she whispered back, "but he's going to act anyway."

"Without crutches?"

"Yes. Anything for art!"

The Nail stuck his head between the two of them. "That's what I call a hearty soul in a healthy body," he whispered.

The lights went down, the curtain went up, and Trym Thomas walked onto the stage with his tiger. "'Now old desire doth in his death-bed lie,'" he said.

Then came the applause. The show had started again.

The quality of the performance was mixed. Sigmund was actually the worst one. He had overestimated his own abilities a bit. Even though he had both adapted the play and acted as the prompter, he wasn't all that confident with his lines. He also had a tendency to recite the parts instead of acting them. He wasn't always sure where he should stand and often went the wrong way, but usually he ended up where he was supposed to be. The Nurse had stopped glaring but kept stumbling around onstage and kept the youngest viewers entertained. Ultimately it was Romeo and Juliet who made the last four acts a success. They played with a youthful innocence that touched the older viewers and inspired the younger ones. Their excellent rapport turned the old play into a performance that even today's teenagers could put up with.

The girls screamed every time Markus appeared, and the boys stared at Ellen Christine with their eyes wide and glazed over.

When they reached the scene where Romeo finds Juliet lying apparently lifeless in the tomb, it was dead quiet in the room.

Markus leaned over Ellen Christine and said:

> *"I will kiss thy lips*
> *Haply some poison yet doth hang on them,*
> *To make die with a restorative."*

He was the only one who saw that she smiled at him and opened her mouth as he kissed her.

They were lying in the middle of the stage with their arms around each other when Turid gave the Prince's last monologue:

> *"A glooming peace this morning with it brings;*
> *The sun, for sorrow, will not show his head:*
> *Go hence, to have more talk of these sad things;*
> *Some shall be pardon'd, and some punished:*
> *For never was a story of more woe*
> *Than this of Juliet and her Romeo."*

The curtain fell. It was still completely quiet in the room. The curtain went up again. Markus and Ellen Christine stood in the middle of the stage holding hands. They bowed.

The first person to stand and applaud was Principal Dahl.

The next day summer vacation started.

CHAPTER 22 The review in the local paper was gushing. It ended like this:

Ellen Christine Holm (Juliet) and Markus Simonsen (Romeo) had such chemistry they rivaled Claire Danes and Leonardo DiCaprio, as was abundantly evidenced by the reaction they got from the younger members of the audience. Of the other actors, I would like to mention Mons Simonsen as the Nurse. In Mr. Simonsen the little town of Ruud has found its own comic genius, on a par with the likes of beloved Norwegian greats Rolv Wesenlund and Aud Schønemann.

After a slightly confusing first act, Sigmund Bastiansen Vik's show grew into a tremendous viewing experience. We are truly sorry that there won't be more performances. Couldn't it be revived this fall? Encore! Encore! Please?

The Four-Leaf Clovers had an end-of-the-year party in their lean-to above the quarry. Mona and Ellen Christine were going to England together on vacation along with their parents. Markus and Sigmund didn't know yet where they'd go, but they hoped they could do it together. It had been two days since the opening, but Markus thought it felt like a year. They ate chocolate and drank cola. None of them said much. It had been a strange time. Now it was over.

Ellen Christine and Mona looked at each other. "Wormster," Mona said quietly, "did you know she's moving?"

Something sank in him. "Oh?"

"Yeah," Ellen Christine said. "She's going to move back to Paris."

What had sunk rose up again. "Oh, you mean Alexandra?"

"Yeah," Mona said. "Her mom found a job there. She wants Alexandra to live close to her dad."

Ellen Christine was looking at him. "Who did you think we meant?"

"I thought you guys meant you."

She smiled at him. "Oh no. I'm going to live here as long as I live."

"Don't promise too much," Sigmund said, taking a drink of his cola.

"Well, I'm going to live here next fall, anyway," Ellen Christine said. "Are you sad about it, Wormster?"

"No, I'm happy about it."

"I mean that she's moving."

He took a bite of chocolate. "I don't know. I haven't thought about that yet."

"Just relax," Sigmund said. "Leave the thinking to me."

"Do you want to be with me this fall, Wormster?" Ellen Christine asked.

He looked at her without answering.

"I mean in the Four-Leaf Clovers," she said.

Markus nodded. "Yeah, we'll be together as long as we live," he said.

"At least almost." She was still smiling.

"I'm happy about that," Markus said.

"Me, too," Mona said. "But now we have to go."

The girls got up.

"Don't go," Markus said.

"We have to pack," Mona said. "We're leaving tomorrow."

"I mean, come back."

"We always come back," Ellen Christine said.

"What about a little good-bye kiss, Lady Montague?" Sigmund asked.

"With pleasure, Mr. Montague," Mona said and kissed him. "Ugh! You taste like chocolate."

Markus and Ellen Christine looked at each other a little hesitantly. The play was over, and they didn't have a reason to kiss each other anymore.

"Have a good summer, Wormster," she said.

"Yeah."

"Do you want me to …?"

"What?"

She looked at him seriously, then she blushed, smiled again, and said cheerfully, "Do you want me to teach you to hug?"

"Yes," Markus said. "I would."

Markus and Sigmund stood outside the lean-to and watched the girls walking away.

"Do you think they'll turn around and wave?" Markus asked.

"Yeah," Sigmund said. "I'd bet on it."

He was right. Sigmund was usually right.

"Bye, Romeo!" Ellen Christine yelled.

"Bye, Juliet!" Markus yelled. "'O, wilt thou leave me so unsatisfied?'"

She smiled and waved. "'This bud of love, by summer's ripening breath, May prove a beauteous flower when next we meet!'" she yelled and disappeared around the bend along with Mona.

"Are you in love with her, Wormster?"

"I don't know what I am."

"No, I'm sure you don't. That's the problem with you, isn't it?"

"No, Sigmund," Markus said, waving to the empty road, "that's the problem with *you*."

When Markus got home, Mons was sitting in the living room, reading.

"Dad?"

"Yes?"

"Do you know she's going to move?"

"Yes. She called and said good-bye."

"Alexandra?"

"No, Sara."

"Oh. Dad?"

"Yes?"

"Are you sad?"

"Why?"

"Because she's leaving."

Mons thought about it a little. "Yeah, because now I'm probably never going to get to play the king's ghost in *Hamlet*. And, hey, did you notice her eyes?"

"No."

"They were different colors."

"Alexandra's, too."

"Yeah," Mons said, nodding. "I figured as much."

"Dad?"

"Yeah?"

"Are you …? Were you …?"

"Was I what, Markus?"

"Oh, nothing."

They looked at each other. They both knew what they were talking about.

"I think maybe I was," Mons said slowly, "but I don't know if I am."

Markus nodded. "That's exactly how I feel, too. Are you reading *The Sorrows of Young Werther*?"

"No," Mons said. "I'm reading *Tarzan of the Apes*. Oh, you got some mail."

"From who?"

"I have no idea, but there are fourteen letters. I think they're from girls."

"Why?"

"Because there are hearts drawn on almost all the envelopes. Here they are."

He gave the letters to Markus, who opened one of them and blushed.

"What does it say?"

"Nothing, Dad. It's just someone who wants a picture of me."

Mons smiled. "Love isn't easy, is it?"

"No, Dad," Markus said. "What a jaunt it is."